SONS OF CAASI
Battle for Time

a novel

by

P. C. GRANT

SPECIAL EDITION PRE-RELEASE

Sevenhorns Publishing
276 5th Avenue, Suite 704
New York, NY 10001
www.sevenhornspublishing.com

Sevenhorns Publishing is a division of SEVENHORNS.
The SEVENHORNS name and logo are trademarks of SEVENHORNS, LLC.

Library of Congress Control Number: 2011914095

ISBN 978-1-734-95272-8 (ebook)
ISBN 978-0-983-84270-5 (hc)
ISBN 978-0-983-84271-2 (paperback)
ISBN 979-8-633-39414-6 (paperback KDP)

Printed in the United States of America.

Sons of Caasi
Battle for Time

Next in the Sons of Caasi Series:

Reign of Deception
Alien Soil
Crimson Web
Rise of Unicus

**Thank you for purchasing a copy of
Sons of Caasi: Battle for Time**
Special Edition Pre-Release

My brother Paul Grant, Jr. died suddenly on New Years' Eve 2019 at age 52. He was the inspiration behind the upcoming Sons of Caasi stories and co-creator of many of the characters. After his sudden and tragic passing, I have decided to release this Special Editor's Edition of the book in his honor.

My brother was a pillar of hope and inspiration for his nieces, nephews, me, and everyone who was blessed to know him. He never married or had any children of his own, but he invested his life in every young person he knew. He was devoted to his nieces and nephews and children of countless friends for whom he was a beloved uncle.

In addition to his responsibilities as chief technology officer for a Massachusetts regional health center, Paul took the initiative to launch a program for local kids to learn about the hospital and be inspired to achieve their dreams.

Though my brother, Paul Grant, Jr. will not see the final publication of Sons of Caasi, your purchase will help support the Grant family's ongoing work of creating and developing the stories we shared as children and building a philanthropic foundation in his name. The foundation will support selfless individuals like him, who are willing to fill the void for fatherless, abandoned, and at-risk children, a cause that was dear to his heart.

For more information please visit:

UnclePaulFoundation.com

Thank you for your support,
Christopher Grant Sr.

To Paul and Secnola Grant
Your love, unwavering support and commitment to the vision
surpasses any earthly parental call.

∞

In loving memory of Paul Grant Jr.

Table of Contents

Table of Contents

Preface

As kids, my brother Paul and I created stories about beings from fantastical worlds with extraordinary powers. For us, running around the house was time traveling at light speed from one dimension to another. Leaping across the space between our twin beds, we surfed intergalactic wormholes connecting planets in far off galaxies. Our made up stories were spontaneous and ongoing, like a cosmic soap opera. Each new episode absorbed us for hours, as though they were reality and the world of our New Orleans neighborhood was not.

We'd launch into an imaginary adventure anytime or anywhere—late at night after our parents prayed with us and shut off the lights thinking we were asleep, or after we'd seen a cool movie, or even during long trips in the car. Occasionally my sister would join us, but she'd always exit once the story lines called for an epic battle. She was too girly for our fight scenes.

Sometimes my parents would overhear us spinning our action-packed sci-fi tales. I just knew they thought we were insane, though they never said so or stopped us. I think they enjoyed listening to our make-believe adventures and reminiscing about when they made up their own stories as kids.

Childlike imagination is necessarily transient, but too quickly the fantasy worlds and superhuman characters of our youth give way to the realities that come with adulthood— and fly out of our lives forever. Like most people, as I got older my mind became filled with the issues of everyday life. School, work, money, and relationships took up permanent residence in my grown-up mind. Before I knew it I was married with two kids of my own. The pretend world that I once escaped to as a child was now seldom visited except for an occasional stroll down memory lane with my brother.

Preface

I found myself—like my parents before me— eavesdropping on the imaginary journeys of my little ones. I often smiled to myself, realizing they had their own unique tales to tell, full of amazing characters and fantastic places I'd never dreamt of. Yet there was always a hero, a great love and an epic rescue that required a tremendous sacrifice. I was captivated by the idea that our youthful desire to create stories might be motivated by something or someone beyond ourselves. Like a super AUTHOR who compelled not just our stories, but maybe every tale ever told.

As I thought about the imaginary adventures of my youth, listened to my kids, and looked at the world around me, my long dormant imagination was sparked to new life. I had a story to tell and decided right off that I would write a novel, but with a background in the music industry and not as a writer I was feeling less than qualified to take on a project of such magnitude. Still, I struggled with an irrepressible urge to tell the tale. Thankfully my wife advised me to just start writing—and I did. Not only is she beautiful and smart, she's my encouragement, too. It also helps that she is the ultimate bookworm! She's passed that gene on to my daughter, who, like most teenaged girls loves a good romance— featuring a drop dead gorgeous guy with excellent abs. My son is the ultimate superhero/action/fantasy buff and loves to create stories almost as much as I do. With the three of them at my side and the support of a host of family, friends, critics and advisors too vast to mention, I confidently invite you to embark on a journey through one of the most thrilling and unpredictable fantasy fiction novels ever imagined. Welcome to the world of Sons of Caasi.

—P. C. Grant

Their World

The FINISHER - The omniscient and omnipotent creator of Spatium and its inhabitants. He has purposed to create a new universe and has chosen the Time-Ruler from among the sons of Caasi to reign over it.

Spatium (Spah-tee-um) - A vast and mysterious world of staggering heights and unfathomable depths, created by the FINISHER in a dimension outside of time and space, Spatium has existed eternities before the creation of our known universe. Its inhabitants are a regal and mystical people whose attributes will determine the properties of earth itself.

Translation - In Spatium there is no death...only birth. Spatian citizens live to fulfill their life's purpose as authored by the FINISHER and revealed in the mysterious book of Fabula and Syuzhet. They are then translated, or joyfully ushered into the presence of the FINISHER. Transfer is a gift to those who have completed their purpose.

Dispatchment - Equivalent to murder or manslaughter on earth; it's when a Spatian's life is unjustly or accidentally taken away at the hands of another, seemingly at the cost of fulfilling their life's purpose.

The Book of Fabula and Syuzhet - Sacred revelation and voice of the FINISHER. It reveals the dictates of his will and predicts the coming of the Time-Ruler, a powerful warrior-king who will reign over all of the FINISHER's new creation.

Principal Citizens

Caasi (Kuh-zeye) - Powerful leader of the Royal Council of Spatium. Father of Sier and Amo.

Sier (Seye-eer) - Firstborn son of Caasi, who by virtue of birth order is expected to fulfill prophecy and reign as Time-Ruler.

Amo (Am-mo) - Second son of Caasi, he is completely left out of the FINISHER's prophecies and subsequently driven to prove his worth to his father and himself.

Riva (Ree-vah) - Outspoken wife of Caasi and mother of Sier and Amo. She has long harbored doubts about which of her sons should assume the role of Time-Ruler.

Spiritus (Spirit-toos) - Respected metaphysical teacher and member of the Royal Council of Spatium. Caasi's best friend.

Rachel - Amo's best friend and daughter of Spiritus. She unwittingly holds the key to Amo's redemption.

Caduceus (Kah-due-shuz) - Seditious member of the Royal Council of Spatium.

Hittitaes (Hit-teye-teas) - Daughter of Caduceus, she is both stunningly beautiful and conniving.

The Sons of Caasi

Chapter 1

The cool air prickled the boys' skin. Rays of the purest white light emanated from the throne room of the FINISHER high overhead, illuminating the cloudy expanse of the sky. Green, yellow, purple, and orange leaves of soaring trees diffused the brightness from above. Beneath their feet, the ground erupted in a profusion of equally colorful grass.

Amo, the youngest son of Caasi, struggled under the weight of his older brother as they wrestled.

"Stop! That's enough! You're hurting me!"

Sier reluctantly let go and stood, a boastful grin of triumph beginning to curl his lips. Caught off guard, he tumbled backward, landing hard as Amo's leg whipped him.

"Oh, okay! Now you're in trouble!" Sier huffed and charged after his smaller, more agile younger brother.

The fight abandoned, Amo ran for the safety of their mother and home. Sier leaped at his back and lifting Amo from his feet, immobilized him in a stranglehold.

"I can't breathe!" Amo gasped, struggling to break free.

"Not again! I won't fall for that twice!" Sier grunted with the effort to restrain Amo. He squeezed harder, sweat stinging his eyes until he realized Amo's body had gone as limp as a rag doll's.

Sier gaped in horrid fascination as the color rapidly drained from Amo's face. Heart thundering, he loosened his grip and dropped his brother to the ground. Fighting panic, Sier stumbled backward, eyes wide. The reality of what he'd done began to crystallize in the dark recesses of his mind.

Sier startled as Amo's eyes flew open. A second leg whip felled Sier like an ax to the base of a top-heavy tree.

"Gotcha again!" Amo raced for home. He was not willing to risk another bout with Sier, who was now bug-eyed with rage.

Sier roared, clawing his way to his feet in pursuit of his brother. He lurched wildly about, searching for anything with which to beat Amo to a pulp. He spotted a long branch hanging loose from a purple tree. His face contorting with the effort, Sier wrenched the thick branch free in mid-stride. He closed the distance between himself and Amo. Mere yards away, he heard his brother's labored breathing. He could see the sinews of Amo's legs straining to stay ahead. Sier raised the branch, poised to swing.

A split second before Sier swung, Amo swiveled his head around to look back. Heart racing, he ducked low, just dodging a blow he was sure would have decapitated him. Amo resumed running in earnest. He was certain Sier was crazy enough to dispatch him, for real.

"Come on, Sier! That's enough!" Amo yelled. "You're out of control!"

Sier, recovered from swinging, was hot on Amo's heels. "I'm sick of you tricking me. Now, you will pay!"

Amo could feel Sier gaining on him. Soon, Sier was close enough to launch the branch at his brother's furiously pumping legs.

Shards of pain shot up Amo's legs. He landed with a thud, and before he could right himself, Sier was upon him. The two brothers grappled in the rainbow of grass, tumbling down a steep incline in a tangle of flailing arms and legs. They reached the bottom with Amo pinned beneath.

"Sier! Sier! Stop it now! Both of you come in to eat!" The familiar sound of a shrill and demanding voice halted the fight.

Sier's raised fist stopped in midair even as he readied a punch to Amo's face. Instead, he punched the ground inches from Amo's head and leaned in close.

"You're weak!" Sier said. "Your mother has saved you once again." Sier stood, eyes narrowed, glaring with contempt. "You could never be Time-Ruler!"

∞

Amo lay panting, pondering his brother's words. He wondered if Sier would one day succeed in dispatching him.

Catching his breath, he squinted at the hazy expanse overhead. The air grew warm around him, and he was mesmerized by the glow from above. Neither the kaleidoscope of leaves in the towering trees nor the haze shaded him from the growing intensity of the light. Transfixed, he had the strange feeling of eyes upon him. He lazily wondered if the FINISHER was watching.

"Amo!" His mother's voice snapped him from the trance. "I will not call again!" she shouted from the house.

Born to Conflict

CHAPTER 2

Sier sat across the well-worn table from his brother Amo. He was the taller of the two, his body thickset and muscular compared to Amo's lean, more angular frame. On many occasions as Fledglings, Sier had bested his brother simply because he was stronger. He subconsciously stretched his legs, comfortable with taking up more space in the room.

"Quit kicking me, lout!" Amo shoved a foot in Sier's direction, upsetting one of two goblets on the table between them.

"Ha! Maladroit!" Sier flicked at the spilled liquid, splashing it on his brother. Amo rolled his eyes and flicked some back.

Their mother, Riva, set heaping plates of steaming food before them and wiped away the mess. The aroma of exotic spices wafted through the room.

"You two can be so uncharitable toward each other," she said. "You're not petty rivals, you're brothers. Behave like it!" Her voice was stern, but she gazed lovingly on each of her sons' faces in turn. They had nearly become men before her eyes. Fraternal twins, she marveled at how different they were from each other in build and temperament.

"Yes, Mother, we are brothers, as always. We're just not Fledglings anymore." Sier grunted, "At least, one of us isn't."

He stared pointedly at Amo, stroking the smooth hairs that

covered his jawline and chin. It amused Sier that Amo's cheeks remained downy, like an infant's, the fuzz sparse in contrast to the glossy richness of his own close trimmed beard.

"Sier is a brute, and he's always thought I was born to play the animal in his hunts," Amo said. He banged his fork against his plate, annoyed by the taunt.

"You are never a challenge, except for your cunning." Sier said. He waved in Amo's direction as though swatting an insect.

"And you are just never a challenge," Amo said. He lurched to his left, dodging the spoon Sier pitched toward his head. His brother had always outweighed him, but Amo had escaped Sier's clutches most of their lives by thinking and moving quicker.

The spoon clattered onto the floor, and Riva spun around to admonish them. "Enough, foolishness! Eat!" She stood, hands on her hips.

Her adolescent sons were about to be presented to all of Spatium at the Unveiling. They would be granted the privilege of choosing wives and professions, yet here at her kitchen table they behaved as little more than children.

"Your father will be home, but he'll only be here long enough to have a meal in peace!" She removed a covered dish from the oven and set it atop the stove. "Caasi is a reading at the Hall of Letters."

"Do you think he'd have me along, Mother?" Amo asked. His eyes begged for a yes.

"I don't see why not," Riva said, nodding her approval. "I'm sure Caasi would be proud to have his sons appear with him at the temple." She reached out to touch her firstborn's shoulder. "Would you like to go also, Sier?"

"No, thanks," Sier answered. "A couple of friends and I are practicing manipulation drills for the Dimensional Games."

He shoveled a forkful of food into his mouth and followed it with a long drink from his cup.

Riva stopped short and sighed, her hands falling from her hips. "You must get your father's permission to participate in the Games. I recall him saying you weren't ready."

Sier turned to face her from the chair. "No doubt you're concerned, Mother, but I've been practicing as much as possible. I believe I'm more than ready."

"Beating up on your brother hardly establishes you as a worthy combatant." Riva raised one eyebrow, her mouth a sarcastic swirl.

"Mother, I mean no disrespect, but how could you gauge my readiness?" Sier asked. "You haven't attended any of my tournaments."

Riva paused. True, she hadn't attended any of the Games, and Caasi boasted lately that Sier's skill seemed to increase at every event. Her own tastes tended toward more cerebral pursuits. Her cheeks flushed with guilt over her disinterest in sport, especially since Sier loved to compete.

"Counselor Spiritus says I am superb for a beginner," Sier said. "I've advanced more than even he expected!" He looked steadily at his brother. "No matter," Sier sneered, roughly pushing his chair away from the table. "I'm used to you favoring Amo's interests over mine." He stood, towering over his mother for an instant before turning to stride angrily from the room.

"Sier!" Riva yelled after him. "Come back here!" But he was gone, the pounding of his footsteps receding farther into the house.

"At least finish eating." She chewed her lower lip, a look of anguish wrinkling her smooth face. "Why does he do that?" She directed the question more to herself than to Amo. "I love you both."

"He's always ready to flare up," Amo scoffed. "He knows you love him. He guilts you into forgetting that he never wants to go to the Hall to hear the readings. Then he stomps off, mission accomplished."

Rising from his seat at the table, Amo walked over to his mother and hugged her.

Riva patted his arm and smiled. "Let me ask your father about the reading."

Disengaging herself from Amo's embrace, Riva tilted her head and closed her eyes. She entered into the trancelike state that connected her with Caasi.

"Hello, Beloved. Are you on your way home?" Riva stood still, her lips not moving.

"Yes, love, soon." The words of her husband, Caasi filled Riva's mind. "Why? Is there a problem?"

"No worries here," Riva responded. "Amo would like to attend the reading with you."

Caasi hesitated, and again his voice reverberated in Riva's mind. His words were clearer than her own thoughts.

"I've just learned I will be here longer than anticipated," Riva heard him say. "I will need to go directly from here to the Hall of Letters. Perhaps Amo can accompany me to another reading. I'll be home soon." He finished speaking, and he was gone. Riva's thoughts were once again her own, the telepathic link broken.

Amo's eyes remained glued to his mother's face.

"Sorry, dear," Riva said. "Your father says he's going straight to the Hall of Letters from his duties. He won't be coming home first." She reached up to pat him on the head. "Maybe another—"

"I'm not surprised!" Amo shoved his unfinished plate away from him. "He probably was headed home until he found out I wanted to go with him," he said.

"Your father realizes how important the prophecies are to you," Riva said, softly. "I'm sure if he could take you to the Hall of Letters, he would."

"I'm beginning to believe he's annoyed by my desire to study the prophecies," Amo said.

Riva gathered the dishes and removed them from the table. She busied herself with tidying up the kitchen, a helpless witness to her son's frustration.

"He is so certain that Sier will be Time-Ruler," Amo said. "He thinks it's pointless for me to even read the prophecies, let alone try to find my place in the FINISHER's plan." He gazed over his mother's head and through an open window. His lips trembled slightly. Sadness pulled the corners of his mouth down.

His words triggered a memory from a faraway place in Riva's mind.

∞

"Oh, Caasi!" Riva cries out, her hands gripping the soft bedding strewn about her. The pain is unbearable. She is sure it is more than she can endure.

"Be strong, my love!" Cassi says. He is near, comforting her, trying to soothe her. "It will all be over soon! Your suffering is not in vain. Be strong and of good courage, Riva!" he says. "We are blessed to be part of the FINISHER's plan."

He dips a cloth in cool water and gently wipes beads of sweat from her brow.

∞

Amo's anxious pleas broke into Riva's memory.

"Mother? Mother! Are you well?" Amo said.

Riva collected herself and refocused her gaze on her son. "Yes. Yes, dear. I'm fine," she said. She took Amo's face in her hands.

"Your father is committed to the FINISHER'S will. Sier is the firstborn," Riva said. "To be Time-Ruler is his birthright."

A Friend Indeed

CHAPTER 3

Amo lay across his bed and sulked over his father's decision to go to the Hall of Letters alone. "Why does father not encourage my desire to study the prophecy? Am I, too, not a son of Caasi?" He sat up and kicked a pillow that had fallen on the floor. "Perhaps if I were as brawny as Sier!" He tossed the pillow in the air several times, punching it as it landed on the bed. "Come what may, I must discover who I am, not perish in Sier's shadow."

Startled by an urgent knocking at the window behind him, Amo caught sight of a darkened silhouette against the light blue of the curtains. Recognizing the outline, he trudged over to the window and peered out. He smiled. His friend Rachel continued her rapid-fire tapping on the glass.

Amo opened the window, and Rachel hoisted her petite frame up and into his room in one swift, smooth motion. The two had climbed in and out of one another's windows almost since learning to walk. They'd been best friends for about as long.

Rachel strode across the room, and with a casual flick of her brown ponytail, plopped into her favorite chair. She placed a finger across her lips and tilted her head to one side.

"Still trying to look cerebral, huh?" Amo smiled.

Rachel flashed him a condescending smirk. "My aim is to give my face some character," she said. "I want people to perceive me as the intellectual that I am." She tried to appear scholarly, but instead dissolved into giggles.

Rachel's laughter was one of Amo's favorite things about his friend. He thought the tinkling sound of it was magical. He'd always found her a bit quirky, but her natural smile and quick wit made them kindred spirits. Amo was a trickster, and Rachel was a fan of his most clever pranks.

As far back as he could remember, Rachel had drawn attention with her oddball clothes and confident attitude. She didn't quite fit the same mold as other girls he knew. Rachel never cared as much as they did about fashionable clothing and silly infatuations. Lately, though, she'd begun to turn heads in a different way. The sound of her voice brought him out of his reverie.

"So, what are you doing?" Rachel demanded with her usual bluntness. She thumbed absently through a book from a small table near the chair where she'd landed.

"Nothing. Just thinking about things." Amo noticed the volume of Spatian history perched precariously on her knees. His thoughts returned to the prophecies and his father.

"Must be sad things. You look sort of glum," Rachel said. "Come on, you can tell me." She studied his face.

Amo had always confided in Rachel. He'd told her countless times how much he hated hunting but wished he loved it the way his father and brother did. He'd even begun to share his disappointment over Caasi's reluctance to search the prophecies with him. For the first time, though, he wasn't sure how much of his growing misgivings to reveal.

"Let me guess, it's your father," she said. She plucked the book from her knees and dropped it on the table with a thud.

"Yes, it's my father," Amo said. He hesitated, then rushed headlong into disclosing his feelings to his closest friend.

"He does not consider me in light of the prophecies," Amo said. "The FINISHER created me as well as my brother. Isn't my stock as valuable as Sier's?"

He dove into the pile of pillows on his bed. "I wanted to go to the Hall of Letters with him," he said, recalling the conversation at the table with his mother. "Then all of a sudden, he had to go directly there from his duties." Amo sniffed, wrinkling his nose in contempt.

"Well, instead of getting angry, why don't you just go there yourself?"Rachel asked.

She seemed to be angling for an adventure, but Amo doubted sneaking into the Hall of Letters was such a good idea. Yet, his father's attitude infuriated him. He resolved to prove himself worthy to be Time-Ruler, even if Sier was the chosen one.

"You can get back before your father ever gets home. He won't even realize you've been gone." Rachel encouraged him, her eyes full of mischief. She'd covered half the room before turning to see if Amo followed.

"Hmm, that may not be a bad idea," Amo said. He didn't take long deliberating. He jumped up and joined Rachel halfway across the room.

"Let's do it!" Amo said. "My mother will be resting until my father returns. We'll leave through the window."

Divided Council

CHAPTER 4

Within the pyramid of the Hall of Letters, the metallic walls of the Great Hall were encrusted with deep green emeralds and diamonds that sparkled in perfection. Thick fog raced across the glass floor like the breath of a giant, making it impossible to see one's feet. Light as from a multitude of suns flooded the temple, blazing in through its apex, far overhead.

Caasi and members of the Royal Council of Spatium sat in the center of the room around a table made of pure emerald. Spiritus, the Counselor, the embodiment of the living bridge between soul and body, was seated to Caasi's left. The statuesque Sophia sat to his right. Her head was slightly inclined. Her penetrating gaze was fixed on an unseen vision. At her elbow, the angelic Malaika stood, a sentinel at the ready. He was prepared, as always to carry the FINISHER's message immeasurable distances beyond this sacred place. Next to Spiritus, the glorious Tomos flashed radiantly, his features as sharp as a double-edged sword. Directly across the table from Caasi, the stunningly beautiful Caduceus sat, aloof. The characteristic, ethereal hum of his being emanated from deep within him.

Caasi rose from the table and crossed the enormous chamber to read from the book of Fabula and Syuzhet. The book rested on a large pedestal at the far end of the room. Its pages were made of a vitreous material flecked with mirrored bits. The pages shimmered and sparkled like the facets of a million diamonds. Caasi approached the pedestal, and the pages seemed at first to quiver, then liquefy into a silvery reflective pool.

Caasi stood still, watching as his image materialized briefly before splintering into a multitude of dancing fragments. He took a deep breath and reached out. He reverently touched a glittering rock next to the book. The fragments coalesced to form written words.

Caasi peered at the writing. He heaved a frustrated sigh.

"All we get are puzzles and riddles," he said, rubbing the creases in his forehead. "The writing has become mere smatterings, a message whose meaning we cannot decipher."

Caasi removed his hand from where it rested on the rock.

"The FINISHER is beyond us and a wonder," he said. "No one can fully comprehend him." He smiled vaguely in the direction of the other Council members. "I do wonder why all the mystery. Are we not his pawns, to move as he pleases?" He addressed no one in particular.

"Why does he not make the prophecy as apprehensible as His presence, in which we live and move and have our being?" Tomos asked.

"We all must be patient," replied Spiritus. "The FINISHER is perfect, as are his prophecies. His words will make sense when his work is complete."

"Perfect?" Caduceus said, slamming his fist on the smooth surface of the emerald table. "More like perfectly misleading! The prophecy calls for the Son of Caasi to be Time-Ruler. How are we to know which of the two is destined to reign?"

The electric hum of Caduceus' being intensified. "It appears there are one too many sons of Caasi," he said. His beautiful countenance morphed into an inscrutable mien. "Shall a father dispatch one of his own sons?" The hum reverberated like ominous laughter.

"The FINISHER is not one of us," Sophia said. "His ways are not ours, and ours are not His." Sophia addressed Caduceus, fixing him in a withering stare. "We must pray that he continues to reveal more of the prophecy."

The humming laughter subsided.

"What of the planets?" Tomos resumed his questioning. "The prophetic words state that the Son of Caasi will covenant a bride, and together they will produce a seed planet full of beings heretofore unknown to us—"

"More meaningless augury!" Caduceus interrupted. "Why must we cling to incomprehensible divinations which have no significance for us?" Rising to his full height, Caduceus towered menacingly above the council.

Eyes smoldering, Sophia rose from her own position at the table. "The machinations of your heart are unwise," she intoned. The chamber resounded with her words.

The electrifying hum resumed, growing stronger.

The Approach

CHAPTER 5

Amo and Rachel set out for the Hall of Letters. The temple rose above the horizon, an enormous pyramidal structure so large it seemed to fill the space between the ground and the glowing expanse. Its gleaming apex could be seen far above the horizon.

They paused to catch their breath, panting from the effort to reach the top of a steep rise. Neither spoke, silently taking in the view of the massive bridge in the distance. Its towers rose to stellar heights, piercing the cottony sky. The seemingly endless span connected Spatium and the Hall of Letters across a dark chasm.

Soon they were scrambling down the far side of the rise and tramping over the flat land between the hillside and the bridge. They were in a deep valley with walls that nearly obscured their view of the Hall of Letters. Only the pinnacle of the giant temple could be seen for most of their trek across the valley, during which they couldn't see the Link at all.

The gentle slope of the ground gradually increased, and soon they were climbing toward the valley's crest. The pyramid shape of the Hall of Letters reappeared in the distance. After a while, they caught sight of the Link itself. It loomed larger and larger as they emerged from the basin.

"It's hard to believe something can at once be so breathtakingly beautiful and strong," Amo said. The intricate, gleaming latticework of the Link rivaled the grandeur of the Hall of Letters.

They jogged the remaining distance through a grassy field. They reached the foot of the ramp, then hurried up a broad incline that led to the deck of the Link.

"Rachel, slow down," Amo said. He stopped short, shielding his eyes with his hand and gazing up at the Link. Its arresting superstructure soared above them. Magnificent towers stretched forward in succession toward the Hall of Letters, while the deck glowed with a milky translucence.

Amo's palms were sweating. His heart pounded, fluttered, and then pounded harder against his ribs. His legs ignored the command to walk from the ramp to the glowing floor of the Link.

"What's wrong?" Rachel asked. She was already ahead of him and moving, unfazed, intent on crossing the bridge as fast as possible.

"I'm afraid this is the first time I've crossed the Link on my own," Amo said. "I've passed over a few times with my father, but never alone..." He shifted from one foot to the other, his voice trailing off.

"I've never crossed it," Rachel said. She walked back to where Amo was standing. "Come on! It'll be exciting!" She grabbed his arm, tugging him forward.

Amo's feet dragged over the ground like bricks. "My father says that those who fall from the Link will be dispatched from Spatium until the Beginning is finished," he said.

"I am aware of the warnings," Rachel said. She let go of Amo's arm. "My father has often spoken of the chasm beneath the Link."

Her voice trembled, and she shuddered at the thought of the dark, gaping abyss beneath the Link. She put a hand on her hip to steady herself. She smoothed her hair, absentmindedly. Sidling closer to Amo, Rachel moved away from the Link and back along the downward sloping ramp.

"Maybe we shouldn't cross," she said.

They stood, unable to decide. Rachel had thought her father's admonishments embellished. Now that she actually stood near to crossing the Link, she began to think Spiritus hadn't merely been trying to frighten her out of attempting it.

Amo was caught between crossing the Link without the guidance of father or mother and heading back for the safety of home. He gazed up at the lofty towers . The massive supports soared out of view.

A dazzling light suddenly enveloped Amo, momentarily blinding him. It seemed to come from every direction and pulsated with a soothing warmth. The knot that had been throbbing in his stomach relaxed, and the sweat on his forehead dried. A refreshing breeze swirled pleasantly about him. Tension flowed out of him in waves, leaving him feeling as though he had been washed clean in the purest water.

His eyes became accustomed to the light, and he looked around for Rachel. She was saying something, turning away from the Link and heading back down the ramp. He reached for her, and instantly the light was gone, sucked away by an invisible vacuum. Gone also was his fear of crossing the Link without Caasi.

Amo strode toward Rachel, his eyes focused, arm extended, hand ready to grasp her arm. He couldn't turn back. Everything in him pressed him forward. He must pass over the Link and journey on to whatever awaited him.

"It's okay, Rachel," he said. "Come on." He caught the sleeve of her shirt, halting her progress away from the bridge.

"You're sure now?" Rachel asked. She noticed something was different about him. He exuded an air of confidence. He certainly wasn't afraid anymore.

Firmly taking her hand, Amo led Rachel back the short distance up the ramp. Together, they stepped into the glow of the Link.

The Link

CHAPTER 6

Walking along the Link, Amo and Rachel were silenced by the remarkable beauty of the gargantuan bridge. Out on the Link, a breathtaking panoramic view of Spatium spread out behind and beneath them. The massive structure hummed steadily, as though with a life of its own. They felt like the strings of an instrument, vibrating as if plucked by invisible fingers. Though the strange vibration troubled them at first, they grew accustomed to it and soon forgot it altogether as they made their way across.

Amo had always traveled the bridge with his father and remembered being carried across in his arms or walking beside Caasi, holding his hand. The Link undulated beneath their feet, the deck rising and falling rhythmically with a life of its own. The air around Rachel and Amo grew misty. It swirled and eddied in pools that formed and dissolved with the wave-like motion of the ground. The breeze intensified as they traveled further out onto the bridge. The smooth swelling of the luminescent deck steadily increased until it heaved and writhed under them.

Rachel caught hold of Amo's hand. With terrified eyes, she searched his face for some sign of assurance.

∞

Amo remembered crossing the Link with Caasi for the first time when he was very small. Passing over had been both exciting and terrifying. The fear in Rachel's eyes reminded him of the sense of dread and panic that had risen in his own body, intensifying to nearly match the writhing of the Link. Then he'd heard his father's voice, calm and steady, soothing the fear that had threatened to overtake his mind. Caasi's words were at once strange, yet familiar. They had quieted Amo's being, firmly directing his mind to focus.

Under the voice of Caasi, like the roar of rushing water, there had been another, stronger, deeper voice—more potent than the undulating waves and more powerful even, than the wind. "Be still," it said. Amo let go of himself, and all was still around him. He and Caasi were once again walking along the gently rolling surface of the Link. White, wispy fog in the distance signaled the end of the ramp and the path to the Hall of Letters.

From then on, whenever Amo crossed the Link with his father he felt completely safe. He was confident he couldn't be lost no matter how windy it became or how vigorously the floor of the, Link surged and swayed beneath them. Always in the turbulence at the center of the Link he would listen, calling out to the deep, trusting the power that always brought him and Caasi safely to the other side.

∞

Now Amo reached out to Rachel with his mind to comfort and reassure her. He wasn't certain she would even understand the soothing words that flowed out from him, encouraging her to focus and to listen. He watched as the terrified expression on her face and in her eyes gave way to one of peace, and then to joy. Holding hands, they emerged from the storm and continued walking along the calm, smooth surface of the glowing deck.

They descended the ramp from the Link. The road before them was shrouded in thick, white fog that swirled gently around their feet. It rolled like fluffy clouds from the base of the ramp and flowed up to the entrance to the Hall of Letters. Drawing closer, Amo spotted two hulking forms stationed on either side of a soaring arch outside the temple court.

"Wait," Amo said. He tugged on Rachel's arm and pointed toward the guards.

"Who are they?" She asked, squinting to get a better view.

"The Protectors. We need to get past them—" Amo said.

"What if they see us?" Rachel said, interrupting him.

He motioned for her to crouch low in the fog next to him. "I've never been here without my father. They probably won't just let us in," he said.

"Well, that's terrific," Rachel said. She flipped a few strands of hair from her eyes.

"How will we get inside?" she asked. "It looks like there's only one entrance." The smooth face of the pyramid slanted up and away, light glinting off its surface.

They remained silent for a moment, brows furrowed. The cool mist ebbed and flowed around them.

"I have an idea." Amo said, face brightening. "Why don't you distract the guards while I sneak in? Once I'm well past the arch and inside the temple, I'll create some kind of commotion to draw them inside." He paused.

Rachel nodded in agreement.

"While they're investigating," he continued, "you follow them into the courtyard. I'll meet you. We'll hide until the Protectors go back out to their posts."

"It's worth a try," Rachel agreed. "Besides, we've come too far to turn around and go home."

Through the Arch and Into the Silvery Wood

CHAPTER 7

Hidden in the dense fog near the entrance to the Hall of Letters, Amo, and Rachel, watched two magnificent beings standing guard in front of the arch.

"Gosh!" Rachel gasped. "They must be at least seven feet tall!"

The Protectors wore breastplates made of shiny glass. Their chiseled arms and legs glistened in the light emanating from the courtyard behind them. Helmets of sparkling glass-covered their heads and faces. Rising above and out to either side, each had a set of large, muscular wings extending from their backs. Their feet were shrouded in the swirling fog.

Caasi often thrilled Amo and Sier with stories of the FINISHER's angels. Amo thought the Protectors must surely be angels.

Amo lowered himself to the ground. He lay flat on his belly, hidden by the heavy mist flowing in and around the temple. He kept out of sight, while Rachel approached the guards.

"Greetings!" Rachel took a deep breath and smiled her most charming smile. She positioned herself in front of the guards. She craned her neck backward to peer up at them. "Uh, I wonder if you might be able to tell me..." she said, praying the ruse would work.

∞

While Rachel rambled on, Amo scuttled past the guards. He kept low to the ground, under cover of the mist.

Once inside, he glanced around. Seeing no one, he trotted off toward the huge scullery. He remembered where it was from the few times he'd visited with Caasi. He crossed the room, skirting tables and carts loaded with bowls, utensils, and various cooking items. Here, the ministers would prepare food for ceremonial banquets, appointed feasts, and other times of worship and celebration before the FINISHER. He surveyed the room, his eyes alighting on precisely what he'd hoped to find.

∞

From inside the Hall of Letters, a loud crashing sound caused the guards to abandon Rachel's amusing attempts at distraction. They raced into the courtyard to investigate.

Rachel paused for a beat, then rushed blindly toward the soft light spilling out from the courtyard of the Hall of Letters. Just as she reached the light, she was seized by the shoulders from behind and steered along a wall before being pushed into a shadowy recess.

"Shhh! Get down!" Amo whispered urgently. His face was tight, a finger against his lips. He pulled Rachel to her knees in the semi-darkness of a dim alcove. They crouched low and waited, listening to the clanging sounds of metal being moved around in the scullery.

"They stack lots of stuff high in there. One little push…" Amo said softly in response to Rachel's quizzical stare.

Their breathing made a loud, whooshing sound in the dark. Catching her breath, Rachel squinted to see beyond the shadows of the alcove and out into the courtyard. The inside of the pyramid was hollowed out. All manner of glittering stones adorned its high walls.. At the center stood a magnificent edifice, fronted by two imposing doors.

"Amo," Rachel whispered, "do you know where you're going or what you're looking for?" She moved her face close to his ear.

"Vaguely," he said, keeping his voice low. "Most of it's familiar from visits with my father. I believe the book of Fabula and Syuzhet is in there." He pointed toward the large building at the center of the court.

Amo and Rachel quieted as the guards emerged from a door in the outer wall. They were marching toward the grand arch.

"Looks like they're returning to their posts," Amo said. "I guess it's now, or never!" He glanced around the courtyard before standing up in the alcove. No sound came from anywhere inside the massive temple.

"We'll cross the courtyard to the outer sanctuary," Amo said.

Rachel stood to her feet beside him, listening.

"From there," Amo continued, "we'll make our way past the conference rooms. My father and the others should be meeting in the Great Hall."

Rachel nodded, and after another quick scan of the courtyard, the two darted across the mist-covered floor to the sanctuary doors. Amo pushed against one of them. It swung quickly, gliding open without as much as a squeak on polished hinges. He and Rachel stepped across the threshold.

"This is the outer sanctuary," Amo whispered. They'd entered a vast hall. Its vaulted ceilings and shimmering walls of white gold met beneath the pyramid's apex. The hall was lit from above by diffused light that radiated through the crystal pinnacle. The light poured into the room like water filling a bowl. A huge arch framed an opening at the opposite end of the hall. Twisting, branching shapes filled its shadowy interior, like trees growing up from the temple floor.

"How beautiful!" Rachel sighed. Her eyes strained to make sense of the twirling, glittering shapes in the distance.

The fog-swirled close to the floor, dancing and flowing around fluted columns flanking the massive doors lining the outer walls.

"There sure are a lot of doors!" Rachel said. She counted seven on each side. They led away from where she and Amo stood toward the opposite end of the chamber.

Amo guided her to the line of doors on their right. "That's the Great Hall," he said, motioning toward the silvery tree shapes. "There, beyond the arch."

They crept down the hall, past six of the seven doors in succession. As they approached the arch, Rachel realized that the shapes were indeed, trees. Their gnarled trunks grew up into spreading branches that sparkled and intertwined, creating a curtain of leafless fingers that clawed the air. The arch itself appeared to be a kind of domed anteroom.

Amo and Rachel could see Spiritus and the other council members seated around a green table. Caasi stood behind a pedestal across the room. They reached the last door and listened, straining their ears to catch the voices filtering through the trees.

"I'll have to leave you here," Amo whispered, indicating a fluted pillar near the last of the doors lining the wall. "You'll be safe and out of sight in case the Protectors come looking for us." He steered Rachel to the far side of the column and motioned for her to step in close between it and the wall.

"I'll need to get closer to hear—" Amo stopped mid-sentence.

Rachel was vigorously shaking her head. "No," she whispered. "Why don't we just wait until they leave, then go in and look at the text?" she asked. Her voice was low and intense.

"I must hear what they are saying regarding the prophecies!" Amo said. He pressed a finger over her lips, reminding her to whisper. "Please, stay here," he insisted. "I won't be long."

"Amo, it's too risky!" Rachel said. "If you're caught, I can't imagine what your father will do!"

"Remember, your father is in there, too," Amo said.

Looking past Amo, Rachel watched her father, Spiritus and the others in deep discussion around the table.

Rachel returned her gaze to Amo's face. "I'd rather get caught and punished than see your father upset with you," she said.

Before Rachel could protest, Amo darted from behind the column, crossed the distance to the archway, and disappeared into the glimmering forest.

Rachel squeezed in close between the pillar and the wall. She considered Amo's words and admitted she didn't want to upset her father, either. For as long as she could remember, they'd been close. Spiritus had taught her many things with patience and love. She admired the breadth of his knowledge and the beautiful simplicity of his wisdom. Her father had a way of explaining things that even a child could understand. The thought of disappointing him saddened her.

She was so careless! Why hadn't she listened to Amo, instead of convincing him to come here?

Hiding in Plain Sight

CHAPTER 8

Amo knelt, hidden among the trees under the cavernous Archway. From where he crouched, he could see Caasi, Counselor Spiritus, and the other council members seated around the large table. His lips curved in a small, satisfied smile. This unexpected excursion was unfolding well.

Caasi's voice interrupted Amo's musings, rising emphatically above the others. Startled, Amo sunk lower and willed himself invisible.

"The birthright belongs to Sier!" Caasi said, addressing the Council. "There is no doubt he is destined to be Time-Ruler."

"Yes, but what of Amo? What is his purpose?" Tomos asked, a concerned expression wrinkling his brow. "Does the FINISHER have no purpose for the second Son of Caasi?"

"Most certainly the FINISHER has a purpose for Amo," Caduceus drawled. "For all, we know he is to be dispatched, sacrificed in a show of unconditional loyalty, perhaps?" he sneered.

"We must seek the FINISHER to gain wisdom regarding the prophecy," Sophia declared. "Arguing over it is of no profit." She directed her gaze at Caasi. "Let us continue this in our next reading, she said."

"It seems we are getting nowhere," Caasi said. He nodded, staring daggers as he sized up Caduceus.

Malaika and the Recorders, Palek, and Rex, murmured their assent.

Caasi closed the sacred book of Fabula and Syuzhet, ending the meeting.

As the others stood to leave, Spiritus approached Caasi. He looked about, making sure no one was within earshot.

"Have you spoken to Sier regarding our agreement?" he asked.

∞

Amo shrank back, deeper into the cover of the trees. He watched the council members exit the chamber through various doors. No one approached the forest under the archway. He marveled at the striking beauty of Caduceus, who remained standing near the table.

His breath caught in his throat as Caduceus seemed to lock eyes with him. Amo's mouth felt as dry as sand.

Caduceus cocked his head to one side. He stared intently, as though straining to distinguish something amid the trees.

Amo's skin crawled. Every hair on the back of his neck stood up, registering the electrically charged air around him. He sensed an ominous presence searching for him in the silvery forest, and the faint notes of an intoxicating melody hummed in his ears. His eyes were riveted on the face of Caduceus. Amo prayed silently to the FINISHER that he was indeed, invisible.

At once, Caduceus, satisfied that there was nothing hidden amongst the trees, gave a slight shrug of his shoulders. He left the hall through one of the far doors.

Amo's breath whistled softly as he exhaled a sigh of relief. He clenched his teeth and tried to calm the tremors that wracked his whole body. His father's voice cut in on his thoughts.

∞

"Yes," replied Caasi. "It's been discussed. And Rachel? You've informed her?" Caasi and the Counselor continued talking as they walked toward the arch where Amo hid.

"Not yet," Spiritus answered. He cleared his throat. "She will not appreciate such an arrangement. She is strong-willed, like her mother."

The two reached the near side of the hall, passing close to where Amo remained hidden.

"I'm convinced her loyalty to Spatium will ultimately win out," Spiritus said.

"These things can be difficult between a father and his treasured daughter," Caasi said, patting his friend's shoulder. "Just know that the sooner she is informed and the betrothal cemented, the better."

The two men exited the Great Hall, leaving Amo alone among the shimmering trees.

∞

Amo's heart raced, and his head was pounding. After a few deep breaths, he opted to proceed as he and Rachel had discussed. He would sort out the details and decide how much to tell her once they'd examined the prophecy. He threaded his way back through the trees and out from under the arch. He crossed the hall to the column where she waited.

"What happened?" Rachel asked.

"Shhh." Amo waved her forward with a hand. He guided her through the shimmering trees and into the Great Hall. The chamber was now empty. The Royal Council of Spatium had dispersed.

Amo approached the book of Fabula and Syuzhet with Rachel at his side. The massive tome was bound in a glowing, vitreous material that beckoned to be touched.

As Amo reached out for the smooth, glassy cover, the book flew open. Surprised, he drew back as the silvery edged pages sped open from right to left. A rush of air flew up from the fluttering sheets.

Suddenly the flurry of activity stopped, and the mysterious book lay flat, splayed open to reveal written symbols that darted back and forth across the lustrous sheets. Slowly, a single set of letters gathered solidly above the center of the book as all the others melted away.

Amo and Rachel stared, open-mouthed.

Sudden Metamorphosis

CHAPTER 9

Under its vaulted ceiling, the large gymnasium of the Axle teemed with magnificent obstacles, targets, and various items for training in combat of every kind. Holograms of exotic creatures stood ready for battle.

Crash! Bam! Swoosh! The sounds of Sier's effort to triumph over a powerful invisible force echoed throughout the arena.

"I must be quicker!" Sier slammed a fist into his palm, unsatisfied with his performance.

"Relax!" Sier's friend, Tilac grabbed towels from a passing steward. He walked over to where Sier stood. "You're too hard on yourself. No one else is even capable of the manipulations you're achieving. You are in fine form for the Dimensional Games." He handed Sier a towel.

Sier grunted. "Yeah, that may be true." He wiped beads of sweat from his forehead with the towel. "But my father won't allow me to enter the Dimensional Games if I don't advance to even higher levels. I must improve!" He stepped backward with one foot, and took a wide stance for balance. "Let's try again!"

He cupped his hands to frame a small tree in a pot on a platform some distance away. A sphere of intense, bluish-white light appeared between Sier's palms, then vanished with a "whoosh." The sphere of light instantly reappeared in the distance and enveloped the tree. The plant withered and wilted, aging until it died, crumbling to nothing.

"Wow! That was amazing! Much better than before!" Tilac cheered. He and Sier walked over to inspect the disintegrated tree. They reached the spot where it had stood, and Tilac leaned in close to examine the remains.

"Unbelievable!" Tilac said. He stared at the ruined plant. "I doubt anyone in the tournament has a chance against you!" He stood up. "You will definitely be a challenge for the mighty Audex, even with his sound manipulations." He paused. "You may even be ready to be the Time-Ruler."

Sier grunted absently. He knelt and poked at the remains of the tree.

"I don't understand this idea of time," Tilac said. "It sounds like the FINISHER's new creation will be a prison." He rubbed the side of his head and scanned the room. The gym was empty.

"My father says living conditions there will be harsh," Sier replied. "Its inhabitants will have bodies that deteriorate. They'll grow feeble and irrational."

"Seems cruel," Tilac said. He poked at the wrecked tree with his foot. "Is that what it will be like to exist in time? Do you think it'll be painful for the poor creatures?" He glanced at Sier.

"I don't know. Let's find out!" Sier abruptly turned to Tilac and cupped his hands as if he held a large ball. The sphere of electric blue light again materialized. Sier hurled the ball.

Tilac's surprised face contorted in agony as he was lifted, screaming, high above the gymnasium floor. His skin wrinkled and contracted. The fluids and muscles of his body emerged and then decayed, falling away from his still moving bones. Tilac's dwindling remains writhed grotesquely, though he was not fully consumed.

Satisfied with the results of his macabre experiment, Sier relented. His eyes aglow with an eery blue light, he revived the decaying flesh, reversing the aging process. He watched as Tilac's mottled form metamorphosed backward through various stages, from rotting corpse to young adult, from prepubescent child to floating embryo. Sier's lips pulled back in a grin.

He tilted his head and nodded, restoring Tilac to his original state. Tilac's exhausted body slumped to the floor. He inhaled deeply, his youthful body revived. He leapt, clawing the air, fully intent on attacking Sier.

Sier pushed a ray of light out from his hands, and Tilac's forward progress was halted in mid-air. Sier yanked Tilac's body back and forth like a puppet's, reversing then advancing his actions over and over again. He giggled as though he were playing with an amusing toy. He replayed Tilac's movements mercilessly. Then, tired of the game, Sier closed his eyes, and in a flash he and Tilac were once again standing on the far side of the gymnasium, appraising the withered tree.

"Wow! That was amazing! Much better than before!" Tilac cheered. He looked uneasily in the direction of the destroyed plant. "Is that what it will be like to exist in time? Do you think it'll be painful for the poor creatures?"

"I don't know." Sier smirked. "You tell me." He jerked his head toward the exit. "Hey, let's get out of here. I think I'm ready."

Gray Storm Rising

CHAPTER 10

Sier and Tilac left the Axle and sauntered along the road leading to Spatium proper. The Axle itself was located outside of the city. The building was set in a clearing amid tall, vividly colored grasses that waved in the breeze. Downpours were common to Spatium, and lush vegetation thrived along the roadside. It began to drizzle as Sier and Tilac walked. Soon they were showered by rain from the glowing expanse above.

Tilac reached into a fold of his clothing and pulled out a small pen. He pointed it toward the clouds, and a transparent canopy expanded overhead, shielding them from the downpour.

Sier smiled at his friend's ingenuity. He made a mental note of Tilac's ability to manipulate the elements. He filed the information away in case it might be useful.

"So, who are you most concerned about in the Dimensional Games," Tilac asked. He stuck the pen back in a pocket.

"No one." Sier said. He kicked a stone as they walked.

"Not even Audex?" Tilac asked, eyebrows raised. "I mean, he is the reigning champion. Don't you think he warrants some consideration?"

Two figures emerged from one of the structures not far from the path. Sier and Tilac stopped talking and gazed at the approaching figures of Hittitaes and her best friend, Serena.

Accustomed to having her way, Hittitaes was known to flash her most charming smile when the need arose, that is, any time doing so would get her whatever she wanted.

They hurried beneath the canopy. The girls crowding into Sier and Tilac under the guise of seeking shelter from the deluge. Hittitaes squeezed water from her thick, auburn tresses, slick with rain. She and Serena stopped to catch their breath.

"Mind if we share your umbrella?" Hittitaes wiped the back of a hand across her forehead. She leveled a beguiling smile at Sier. Her grey, almond-shaped eyes perfectly mirrored the color of the sky.

"Sure!" Sier said, bowing toward Hittitaes. "To deny you anything would be criminal."

"Thank you," Hittitaes said.

"Are you guys coming from the Axle?" Serena asked. She tucked her short, blonde hair behind her ears.

"Yes," Tilac said. He enlarged the canopy slightly as the four of them strolled along the path. "Sier is training for the next Dimensional Games."

"How exciting," Hittitaes crooned. "I'm sure you'll look spectacular—I mean, do well in competition." She drew out the words in a singsong voice.

"What about you Tilac?" Serena cast a flirtatious glance in his direction. She rolled her eyes and mimicked Hittitaes' lilting voice.

The foursome laughed and chatted amiably as they walked along the road. They reached the outlying area of the city where many Spatians lived in large, gleaming dwellings interspersed amid dazzling foliage. The downpour had diminished to a steady drizzle. As far as they could see, the buildings and terrain glittered with refracted light. The broad path branched off into various tributaries, each peppered with stately Spatian dwellings.

The group reached a spot where the path divided. An offshoot snaked along the hillside. A magnificent structure stood ensconced among the trees, not far in the distance.

"We've arrived. Thanks, gentlemen," Hittitaes said. "Let's go, Serena!"

"Thanks, Tilac," Serena smiled as she and Hittitaes stepped out from the shelter of Tilac's canopy.

"Wait," Sier said. He grasped Hittitaes' hand and leaned in close. "We should walk you to your door."

"How very sweet." Hittitaes tossed her hair and stared into Sier's eyes.

"But not now. I wouldn't want my father to get the wrong impression." She stretched up on her toes to peck Sier on a scruffy cheek. Blushing, she grabbed Serena's hand, and the two ran off toward her house.

∞

Tilac grinned as he and Sier watched Hittitaes and Serena disappear onto Caduceus' property. They abandoned the cover of the canopy and continued walking along the path.

"Wouldn't you just love to escort her to the Unveiling!" Tilac laughed. He was confident he already knew the answer. He could drown in the depths of those limpid gray eyes.

"Well, yeah, that's my plan." Sier searched the road for another stone. "Unfortunately my father has made a treaty with Counselor Spiritus. Their plan is for me to covenant with Rachel." He found a speckled rock and kicked it a ways down the road. "I won't be escorting anyone but her."

"Rachel?" Tilac exclaimed. "You're not serious?" He couldn't hide his disbelief. "Rachel is... different. Why settle for her, when it's obvious Hittitaes likes you?"

"My father feels that a treaty between our families will cement Spatium's alliance to the FINISHER and ensure fulfillment of His prophecies." He picked up another rock and sent it soaring out of sight. "The agreement will guarantee the stability of Spatium."

"What about you?" Tilac hurled a stone of his own. "What do you want?"

Sier was silent for a long moment. "I believe the prophecy has its place." He measured his next words carefully. "But I question its credibility in some things."

Along Family Lines

CHAPTER 11

"Would you like something to drink, dear?" Riva asked. "It might help you relax."

Caasi and Riva sat facing one another in cushioned chairs on a large terrace. Numerous residences spread out below and on either side of their own, dotting the landscape down to the edges of the city.

"You seem lost in the deepest of thoughts," Riva continued, her initial query evoking no response from her husband. Getting up from her chair, she walked over to an ornate sideboard. She poured a dark, rich liquid into two glasses.

"Anything you'd like to talk about?" She brought over the glasses and offered one to Caasi.

"Well, I believe Sier is ready to take part in the Dimensional Games," Caasi said. He accepted the drink and patted her hand in thanks.

"Are you certain?" Riva said. She took a long sip of her drink before going on. "Those competitions can be dangerous. Poor Lamec was dispatched in the last tournament."

"Yes, I'm aware of the danger," Caasi nodded. He allowed his gaze to wander over the gently sloping hills. The light rain had given way to a crisp breeze that rustled the high grass.

Caasi turned to face his wife's questioning stare.

"Nevertheless, I truly believe Sier is ready for the Games," he said. "He's been training relentlessly at the Axle."

Riva opened her mouth to protest, but Caasi slowly raised a hand, momentarily halting her objection.

"On several occasions, I've observed him discreetly," Caasi said. "He is mastering his skills quite well." He lowered his glass, setting it on the table. "Who knows when the FINISHER will summon Sier to reign as Time-Ruler. He must be ready."

"I trust you will make the right decision when necessary," Riva said. She rubbed the rim of her glass with a finger. Her words were tinged with frustration.

"Is there a problem?" he asked.

The displeasure in his wife's voice was a familiar sound to Caasi's ears.

"Yes, Caasi!" Riva took a deep breath and allowed the words to leave her in a rush. "The FINISHER has gifted you with two wonderful sons. How can you so completely favor the one while entirely overlooking the other?" She let the question hang in the air. "One of your sons seems to be of so little importance to you." Her voice was flat.

Caasi leaned forward in his chair before answering.

"You refer to my sons as a gift," Caasi said, "but what type of gift brings so much confusion and pain? I love them equally, but unfortunately, only one can be Time-Ruler." He pounded the arm of the chair with a fist. "May the FINISHER help the other!"

His wife tossed her head. She leaned forward as well, jabbing the table with her index finger. "Would Sier even trouble himself to seek the will of the FINISHER?" Riva asked.

They faced each other in the soft light, anger rising between them.

"The FINISHER has chosen one and made no mention of the other," Caasi said. "That is something we both have to come to grips with!"

"The FINISHER has chosen? Or you have chosen?" Riva spat the words.

"Do you think I have not felt the confusion? The resentment?" Caasi asked. "It's a living thing separating us!"

Their eyes were locked, faces set. Caasi straightened in his chair, his back stiff. He appeared majestic, like a king about to issue a proclamation. He delivered his next words with practiced precision.

"Sier is the first born," he said. "To be Time-Ruler is his birthright. He has been given the skills and abilities to fill the role."

"Sier has skills and abilities?" Riva asked. Gesturing with a hand, she rolled her eyes upward before bringing them back to focus on her husband. "Do you know anything of Amo's skills?"

She didn't wait for his answer. "I'm sure you do not! You rarely take notice of him! Are you even aware of his passion for the things of the FINISHER? Have you no regard for his belief in the prophecy?"

"Sier is a warrior, like his father," Caasi said. "He possesses the strength and power to reign as Time-Ruler!"

"Amo is more like you than you care to admit! He desires to discern the meaning of the FINISHER's words," Riva said. "A true warrior-king rules not by power nor by might, but by the essence of the FINISHER! Do you fear that in choosing Amo, you will make a mistake?" she asked.

"It is my decision to make!" Caasi said. "A mistake will be the

FINISHER's to correct. I must do as the prophecy commands! I will not go against what is written."

"I mean you no disrespect, but you have a singular vision when it comes to your sons," Riva said. "You see what you choose to see.

"You speak of confusion and pain. You are not alone!" Her eyes were lightning flashes in a roiling storm. "I suffered the pain of their struggle long before you were ever blessed to lay eyes on them!"

Riva brought a hand to rest on her abdomen, remembering the tempest that once raged there. She could still feel the taut skin of her swollen midsection rippling as the babies wrestled inside.

Of Love and Sacrifice

CHAPTER 12

Sier entered the house from below the balcony. His parents were arguing, but he couldn't make out what they said. His name and his brothers were spoken often. He dropped his shoes and bag in the outer hall and padded into the kitchen. Lately, his father and mother argued a lot about him and his brother. His mother wished Amo had been born first, that he would claim the birthright. Amo was her favorite. But Sier was both firstborn and Caasi's favorite. He loved his mother, but this was a battle she would lose. Their arguing did not matter. He was confident his fate as Time-Ruler was sealed.

Caasi left the balcony and walked downstairs in the direction of his study. He caught sight of Sier just as a door slammed somewhere in the rooms above.

"What's bothering Mother?" Sier asked. He stood at the far end of the hallway, finishing a snack. He'd heard the slam, too.

"Nothing," Caasi said. "She'll be fine." Caasi motioned with his hand for Sier to join him. "Come, sit with me. We must talk."

They entered Caasi's study. It was an enormous room, lined with shelves of books from floor to ceiling. A decidedly masculine space, little touches of Riva's made the room a cozy, inviting haven. Caasi loved his study. He loved the hours spent there alone with his wife, talking, laughing, reading. When the twins came, they moved their activities to the larger family room, but this was still a special place of communion for them. He wondered how long it would be before they met here again.

Sier watched as Caasi sat down behind his desk. He shifted a stack of books to one side. He fidgeted in a seat opposite his father, as anxious as a Fledgling boy. He suspected Caasi's desire to talk with him had something to do with his parents' arguments over which of their sons should be Time-Ruler. He and his brother were like opposite ends of the same rope, with their parents pulling from both sides. He figured one day the rope would break. Amo would end up on Riva's side, and he'd land on Caasi's.

He took a deep breath, steadying himself. He respected his father and trusted that whatever was on his mind, Caasi would treat him with fairness and respect. They were kindred spirits, hunters, and warriors with an eternal code of honor. Caasi played by the rules. Sier knew the rules favored him.

"So, Father, is there a problem?" Sier asked.

Caasi ignored the question. "I've noted your dedication to preparing for the Dimensional Games," he said. "Your skills are quite remarkable. I believe you are ready to compete."

Sier beamed with pride. He jumped up from his seat and pumped his fist. "Yes! Finally, you see what I've been saying all along!" he said. "Thank you, Father!"

"Remember, my son," Caasi said. "You are firstborn in the line of Caasi."

Sier composed himself, his expression sober. "I won't disappoint you, Father. I promise," he said.

"Moreover," Caasi stood and walked around the desk to place both hands on Sier's shoulders. "You have an esteemed birthright."

Caasi stared into his son's eyes, searching in vain for some visible sign, some stamp of the FINISHER's approval on Sier's soul. "The FINISHER has chosen you to be Time-Ruler," he said.

∞

Hittitaes closed the door behind her. She twirled around the grand entryway, dancing and swaying on her heels in the arms of an imaginary partner.

"Who was that walking with you and Serena in the rain?" Caduceus asked. He knew full well who had walked his daughter home.

Hittitaes inhaled sharply, halting her dance in a mid pirouette.

"Father! You startled me!" She met Caduceus as he stepped from a sweeping staircase onto the tiled floor.

"No one important," she answered. "Sier and Tilac graciously offered the shelter of their canopy from the rain." She smiled, her cheeks flushed from dancing.

"I wouldn't call a son of Caasi unimportant," Caduceus said. "His family wields much power in Spatium by virtue of their role in the FINISHER's prophecies." He draped an arm around his daughter's shoulders. They walked farther into the house.

"Of course, I'm aware of their prominence concerning the prophecies." Hittitaes said. She tossed her dark hair, her chin jutting forward with confidence. "Only a fool would be ignorant of the promise attached to Sier and his birthright. Every girl in Spatium vies shamelessly for the slightest bit of attention from the predestined Time-Ruler."

Hittitaes considered herself without competition in this regard, especially if she'd read Sier right on the way home in the rain. Her instincts told her she had.

"You are very astute, my dear," Caduceus said. "My concern isn't for the prophecy as much as it is for my position on the Council of Spatium. And for your benefit, of course."

"A permanent relationship with Sier would make me highly favored, indeed!" Hittitaes said, laughing. Her eyes sparkled, full of mischief.

Hittitaes' stunning beauty struck her father as always. She was the exact image of her mother.

"I assume you're fond of this son of Caasi," he said. He stroked the close beard covering his chin.

"I daresay I had not considered him a potential suitor," Hittitaes said. She fluttered her dark lashes, looking up at Caduceus with wide, innocent eyes.

Her father saw through the lie.

"In that case, the rumor of a treaty between Caasi and Spiritus via the marriage of Sier to Rachel will be of no concern to you," he said. Caduceus watched as his words had the desired effect.

"Rachel?" Hittitaes asked. Her face drained of color as she spoke. She clenched her hands into fists at her sides. The thought of a rival for the coveted status of wife of the Time-Ruler had never occurred to her. The idea of her witless opponent gaining the upper hand through a contrived political alliance infuriated her.

"What would Sier ever want with the likes of her?" she asked.

"Agreed, my dear," Caduceus said, "you far surpass even the most desirable Spatian women in both beauty and intellect. The indomitable Sier would do well to have you as his bride."

Caduceus took his daughter's hands in his own. "The Royal Council of Spatium would do equally well to anoint a leader unconstrained by fear to cryptic, unintelligible prophecies," he said.

"I will do anything to help you, Father," Hittitaes said.

"My dear daughter, Sier may be tempted by Caasi's and Spiritus' proposal," Caduceus said. He lightly patted the top of her head, much as he had when she was a Fledgling girl. "Though, perhaps we can put forth a more enticing option of our own," he said.

∞

Rachel's head was spinning. Hot tears welled up in her eyes, threatening to spill over and run down her cheeks.

"You are betrothed to Sier."

Her father's words echoed in her mind with devastating finality. She was not her own. Had she no choice but to honor the covenant her father had made?

"You are betrothed to Sier."

And what of her growing feelings for Amo? Since that moment on the Link, thoughts of him continually surprised and delighted her. Had he felt it, too? Didn't what she wanted count for anything?

"You are betrothed to Sier."

Rachel sighed. Her father often reminded her, selfish ambition on the Royal Council had nearly devastated Spatium in the First Rebellion. How could she stand in the way of a treaty to prevent another? She was honor-bound to do her part. Still, she wrestled against the urge to rebel.

She longed for the comforting presence and wise counsel of her mother. But Aurora had already been translated to the FINISHER.

Rachel drew the back of her hand across her eyes, wiping away the tears. Aurora would have reminded her that great love sometimes requires even greater sacrifice.

Rachel resolved to ignore the desire of her heart. She would take up the mantle of duty to Spatium and her father. She would marry

Sier, and never reveal her feelings for Amo. She would submit to the will of the FINISHER.

But for now, she buried her face in a pillow and let the sobs come.

The Dimensional Games

CHAPTER 13

"Welcome, honored citizens, to the Spatian Dimensional Games, where feats of raw power and cunning demonstrate the courage and resolve of Spatium's finest warriors!" announced Caden, Keeper of the Dimensional Games.

A vast geological formation provided the perfect natural amphitheater for the tournament. Tiers of seats hewn from solid rock ascended the walls at a gentle angle from the flat bottomed depression. Members of the Royal Council of Spatium and their guests enjoyed the festivities from arcaded boxes semi-circling the top of the arena.

"Who will be Champion of these Dimensional Games?" Caden posed the question to the spectators. Their answer was an cacophony of cheers as the challengers entered the arena.

"Spatians! Salute the combatants!"Caden said. The crowd stood to its feet, erupting in thunderous applause.

Caden bowed with a flourish. "All hail the reigning Champion, Audex!" he said.

Audex swaggered in and mounted the center stage to the loud cheering of his fans.

"And now, greet the returning challengers, Lexicon, Motif,

Biro, Radient, and Staton!" Caden announced the challengers as they entered the arena. Each one charged the field, and after saluting the champion, Audex assumed his respective place on the raised platform.

The stadium floor reverberated with the stomping of a multitude of Spatian feet.

"Ladies and gentlemen, making his debut as a warrior-combatant at these Dimensional Games," Caden announced, "welcome, Sier, Son of Caasi!" The roar of the crowd rose to a deafening crescendo.

Sier sprinted onto the field, waving to the adoring fans. His eyes found Hittitaes in one of the gilded spectator's boxes. He bowed gallantly in her direction. After a cursory nod to Audex, he trotted onto the platform to stand with the other challengers.

"Let the Games begin!" Caden shouted. A shower of confetti deluged the platform. A phalanx of musical, living things erupted in fanfare. The Spatian flag waved in the breeze.

Daphne, Lower Official of the Dimensional Games, took her position on the field. A former combatant, her lithe, muscular frame and disarming quickness made her a formidable opponent. She had nearly bested Caduceus in a match, but his superior tactical skills ultimately won out. Daphne and her team would monitor the competition and settle any disputes. Issues that could not be resolved by her on the field of combat would be referred to Caden, Daphne's counterpart on the Royal Council of Spatium. Together, they comprised the office of Keeper of the Dimensional Games.

Each of the seven combatants employed their unique metaphysical gifts. They battled to overcome obstacles, tasks, and creatures bent on hindering their progress or dislodging them from the course altogether. Lexicon and Staton were ejected mid-course, unable to prevail over the grueling battles.

Biro, Radient, and Motif struggled valiantly onward through clashes with formidable brutes bent on proving their mettle as Spatium's stout-hearted warriors. The solitary figure of Motif emerged from the fray to move on to the next round of the competition.

Audex and Sier each triumphed over equally rigorous trials. They would face each other and Motif in the last rounds of battle. Only the Champion would emerge.

The solemn peal of an enormous bell signaled the beginning of the final rounds of the Dimensional Games.

Sier, Audex, and Motif circled warily, feinting and sparring as they jockeyed for position. The three combatants sized one another up for the initial attack.

Audex suddenly initiated a sound wave that hurled Sier and Motif toward opposite corners of the arena. Both writhed in pain.

Disoriented, Sier saw the crowd standing, mouths open wide and cheering, but he heard nothing. The ground trembled under the pounding of innumerable feet in the stands, but the stadium remained blanketed by an eery silence.

At once, it dawned on him. He was deaf, his ears overwhelmed by Audex's flood of sound. He vaguely hoped his hearing loss was temporary. Glancing to his left, he noticed blood seeping from under Motif's hands, which were clapped tightly against the sides of his head. Sier closed his eyes and ignored the trickle of blood, beginning to flow from his ears.

Audex, certain Sier was at least momentarily out of the fight, strode purposefully toward Motif.

∞

Tilac and Raze took in the contest near each other in the boxes designated for Albar, Captain of the Protectorate, and Game Keeper, Caden. They sat glued to the opening of the battle, "Audex is one tough competitor," said Raze. "Do you still think Sier can beat him?"

"I've seen some of what Sier can do," Tilac answered. "Audex has his work cut out for him."

"Come on, Sier!" they yelled.

∞

"Oh, no! He's hurt!" Hittitaes cried. She craned her neck to see better, but she was certain there was blood coming from Sier's ears. She, Serena, and Melanie occupied Caduceus' box.

"I can't watch!" Serena said, covering both eyes with her hands.

"Well, I, for one, think he could use some encouragement!" Hittitaes declared. She, Melanie, and the others began chanting, "Sier! Sier!"

Serena joined the cheer, but only peeked through her fingers.

∞

Hearing the chant, Rachel and Amo spotted Hittitaes and the others, seated several boxes to their left. "I guess Hittitaes is anything but shy!" Rachel said. Her mouth twisted in a wry smirk.

"Yeah. Tons of guys would give a right arm to hear her chanting their name." Amo, visibly distracted, ran a hand through his hair.

"Seriously?" Rachel stared at him, the meaning of his reaction dawning on her. "You like her! Don't you?" she asked incredulously. "Of all the shallow—ugh!" She tossed her head, obviously annoyed. "Well, she seems to be a fan of your brother! Look at her!"

They both observed Hittitaes leading the rallying cry.

"Sier! Sier! Sier!" came the shouts from where they sat.

"She's just caught up in the competition," Amo said. He waved a hand dismissively in Rachel's direction. "She's way too civilized for him!"

A collective moan escaped the crowd, and they turned back to the match.

"I can't believe Motif is already out!" Amo exclaimed.

Cheers went up as game stewards dragged Motif off the competition field. A second blast of Audex's sound wave at point-blank range had finished him.

"Ladies and gentlemen, only one battle remains to determine our champion!" GameKeeper Caden announced. "Spur the victor on to triumph!"

Throughout the stadium, shouts of "Audex, the Champion!" and countering cries of "Sier! Sier! Sier!" erupted as the last two combatants faced each other for the title of Champion of the Dimensional Games.

"Hmm, it seems your brother's got his eyes on his personal cheering section," Rachel said. She pursed her lips and pointed. Sier was gazing up from the arena floor.

At that instant, Audex shaped his mouth into a perfect circle and emitted a concentrated stream of sound. Superheated molecules of air glowed red, a visible beam that shot across the field and caught Sier by surprise. The shaft of light bored through his midsection. He dropped like a stone, his eyes wide and hands clutching his stomach. The arena went silent. Sier's gasp of pain filled the arena, and rose toward the open sky.

"No, this can't be happening!" Amo jerked his head toward the sound of his mother's cries.

∞

Above the tiered seats, Caasi and Riva had also observed the scene from their spectator's box. White-knuckled, they stared in horror at the body of their firstborn son lying motionless on the floor of the arena.

Riva buried her head in Caasi's chest. Her sobs tore through the air, echoing and drifting away like the confetti floating on the breeze.

Spiritus, Sophia, Caduceus, and the other council members all stood, awaiting the signal that could confirm their worst fears.

The crowd looked on in silence, stunned by the thought slowly dawning in everyone's mind. Sier Caasi had been dispatched.

∞

Sier had been slowly getting to his feet while Audex was making quick work of Motif. Still dazed, his hearing had begun to return. He was intoxicated by the sound of the crowd chanting his name. He allowed himself a split-second glance at Hittitaes in the stands. Distracted by the vision of her cheering him on, he had just caught sight of Audex when a super-heated laser came hurtling across the field. Sier gulped in surprise as Audex's blow struck his mid-section and knocked him to the ground. He lay stunned as the sound of his mother's anguished cries reached his ears. A small smile formed on his lips. He felt his body absorb and then transform the energy of the sound wave. While Audex advanced steadily toward him, Sier lay motionless, gathering his strength.

∞

Audex relished the wide-eyed look of surprise that had convulsed Sier Caasi's face when the bolt of sound struck him. He had noticed Sier's fascination with Caduceus' daughter Hittitaes at the start of the tournament. In a stroke of good fortune, the beautiful Hittitaes had diverted Sier's attention long enough to allow him to land a debilitating blow. Now, as he advanced upon the still form of his fallen challenger, Audex was confident he would retain the title of Champion of the Dimensional Games.

∞

Sier watched coolly as Audex confidently approached. In a flash, he curled his body forward and launched a pulsating sphere of electrical energy from his hands. The sphere slammed into Audex, stopping him in his tracks. Then it enveloped him, lifting him from the arena floor. Sier slowly regained his feet and, with a motion of his outstretched, arm raised the sphere with Audex inside.

The crowd cheered wildly, exhilarated by Sier's unexpected rally and the astonishing turn of events. Their chant surged to a deafening roar while Audex pressed against the electrified bubble, his attempts to escape in vain.

Gamekeepers Daphne and Caden signaled the end of the

championship round. To thunderous applause, they declared Sier the victor.

∞

One by one, the competitors of the Dimensional Games lined the colorfully lighted dais to receive their medals. Caden and Daphne, Keepers of the Games, placed ribboned medallions around the combatants' necks. Motif received the third-place award and Audex, the second.

The colored lights of the platform shifted to white, and Sier made his way forward. Caden and Daphne pronounced him the victor and new Champion of Spatium's Dimensional Games.

Shouts of euphoria went up all over the arena. Tilac and Raze clapped one another on the back. "I told you he'd do it!" yelled Tilac.

"He's just amazing, isn't he?" Hittitaes raved. Serena and Melanie embraced her and joined the cheer.

"Did you think he could do it?" Rachel asked Amo.

"To be honest, I wasn't sure," Amo replied. "But, I'm glad the fool didn't go and get himself dispatched!" He and Rachel laughed and joined in the celebration.

Caasi stood, proudly applauding his son's achievement.

The roar of the crowd rained down on the platform. Sier basked under the deluge of praise.

Enticing Entanglements

CHAPTER 14

The crowd poured out of the stands and surged onto the arena floor to greet the combatants at the close of the award ceremony. Sier was holding court in a cordoned off section of the stadium that quickly overflowed with clamorous fans.

Counselor Spiritus and Tomos came forward to congratulate Caasi and Riva on Sier's win.

"It was definitely suspenseful, but I'm thrilled he was victorious in the end!" Caasi remarked, thankful the tournament was over.

"Suspenseful?" Riva touched a hand to her heart at her husband's comment. "I thought for sure he'd been dispatched!"

Sophia and Malaika joined them, each offering congratulations. They, too expressed their relief that Sier hadn't lost his life in the Games.

Not far from where they stood, Amo caught sight of Hittitaes. She was smiling and nodding politely as her father Caduceus talked with another high ranking denizen of Spatium.

She noticed Amo staring and returned an imploring look with her eyes. "Rescue me!" she discreetly mouthed the words.

Amo looked around, certain Hittitaes was entreating someone else with her hypnotic stare. No, she had definitely singled him out to come to her aid. Giddy with excitement, Amo picked his way through the crowd. Along the way, he gathered his nerve.

"Hi, I'm Amo," he said as he approached her.

Hittitaes leveled him with a smile. "Nice to meet you," she said, playing along with the joke. She excused herself from her father and his guest with a promise to rejoin Caduceus before leaving the arena.

"Your brother did an excellent job in the Games," Hittitaes said, turning to Amo. "He will make a magnificent Time-Ruler."

She slipped an arm through Amo's and steered them both through the crowd. Too late, Amo realized they were heading toward Sier, who was still smiling congenially, accepting congratulations from the crowd.

Amo stifled a sigh. It was obvious that Hittitaes was probably more interested in getting close to Sier than in getting to know him.

"Yes, my brother fought and strategized well. He proved that there may well be a brain woven in amongst all that brawn," Amo said.

"Would I be correct in surmising that you, Amo Caasi, are the intelligent twin?" Hittitaes asked.

Her eyes held him, a spark of something igniting in their depths. Calculation? He wondered. He felt she had weighed him in a balance and found him—

His thoughts were interrupted as Sier rudely stepped between them, encircling Hittitaes' waist possessively with one arm and nudging Amo away with the other. The crowd widened, pressing Sier to give an impromptu victory speech.

"Dear friends," he began, " I am indeed honored to emerge as the champion of these Dimensional Games!"

A cheer went up from the crowd as Sier continued, "On this auspicious occasion, you have witnessed but a glimpse of my ever increasing abilities! As Time-Ruler, I will reign over the new creation with supreme authority granted by the FINISHER Himself! His power is being perfected in me!"

The crowd roared its approval.

"There are tremendous blessings in store for the one who would be my wife!" Sier continued. He pulled Hittitaes close, kissing her ardently in front of the wildly cheering crowd. Handfuls of brightly colored confetti showered them as they parted.

Serena and Melanie cast insinuating glances in Rachel's direction.

"Will your brother be your side kick?" Came a taunt from the crowd.

Sier reluctantly returned his attention to the group. "I alone am chosen to be Time-Ruler," he smirked, "but I'm sure my little brother will be glad to serve me in some lesser capacity."

∞

Sier escorted Hittitaes to her father. He had charged Amo with locating Caasi and Riva. He headed for his private preparation room to refresh himself and change clothes before rejoining his family to go home.

He opened the door and stepped inside. Sier gasped in surprise, startled by the white glare of a brilliant being standing in the center of the room. Its skin reminded Sier of the purest white ivory plants that grew in his mother's garden. Long silken hair shone like gold around its face, which was covered by a mask. The eye-holes were twin abysses of inky black.

"Who are you?" Sier demanded, even as the hair stood up on the back of his neck.

The glowing creature did not respond or acknowledge his presence.

A little unnerved, Sier nevertheless tensed, readying himself to battle the mysterious stranger.

"What are you doing here?" Sier shouted. "This is a private room!" He circled warily, angling for the best position to attack, or defend himself, should it become necessary.

The being put forth a hand, almost gently, and Sier was stopped in his tracks, held fast by an invisible vise-like grip.

"At ease warrior seed of Caasi," the being said. "You need not be afraid." The corners of its mouth warped into the curve of an icy, confident smile. "Rest assured, I have not come here to battle you, but to reveal your true destiny."

Sier remained motionless, comically halted in midstride. He found his position anything but amusing. He grunted, eyes locked on the visitor's face, and listened. He had no choice.

"You are a valiant warrior. You deserve to reign as the most powerful leader of Spatium," the stranger said. "But even the lofty mantle of Time-Ruler brings its own burdens to bear upon your shoulders, does it not?"

The air around the being shimmered in the dim light of the preparation room.

Unbidden thoughts of Hittitaes filled Sier's mind. The fullness of her lips, the soft curve of her neck, her dark, flowing hair and luminous eyes were before him, vivid enough to touch.

"I see that you have a fondness for the beautiful Hittitaes," the stranger remarked, as though reading his mind.

Suddenly, the image of Hittitaes froze and shattered. It was replaced by another, slowly materializing in its place.

"But your father would have you bond with another for the

security of Spatium and out of loyalty to the FINISHER," the stranger said.

The picture in Sier's mind cleared as the voice of the stranger went on. He strained to make out the features of the face before him, but Sier knew who it was. His stomach somersaulted in rejection.

"But that's not your desire, is it?" the stranger taunted.

"What do you want?" Sier roared in frustration. He struggled in vain against the invisible grip immobilizing him. His deepest thoughts lay bare before the stranger.

The creature was unperturbed. "What if I could show you not just how to rule time, but how to become like the FINSHER, perhaps even how to usurp His power for yourself?" it asked.

"You're insane!" Sier sputtered.

"And you're an insolent, brutish child!" The creature spat the words like venom. "The power of Time-Ruler lies not only in the prophecies revealed in the book of Fabula and Syuzhet! These are merely the beginning!"

Sier's eyes widened in disbelief.

"You would be content to be spoon-fed power like an infant," the creature said, " but I offer you hidden knowledge that even your exalted father Caasi withholds! Knowledge that will free you from his control and truly make you the supreme ruler of Spatium and sovereign over all the FINISHER creates!"

Sier stopped struggling. Initially stung by the stranger's insults, now he listened, enticed by the promise of ultimate rule and freedom from his father's dominance.

"The book of Fabula and Syuzhet can be interpreted and used to rule without the FINISHER!" the stranger said.

Sier recoiled. Did he dare think it? Power to rival that of the

FINISHER? The very idea terrified him. It was sheer blasphemy. He ignored his feelings of foreboding, and continued to take in the stranger's words.

"Three metasymbols, once united will reveal the hidden meaning of the Book and unlock its final mystery and power!" The blasphemer continued, "Spiritus holds one of the three. The other two are secreted away in the Hall of Letters. Once the symbols are united, the power of the prophecy will be revealed."

"My father will not tolerate such rebellion!" Sier threatened, wavering between his own lust for power and loyalty to his father and his father's beliefs.

"Caasi is a fool!" The stranger mocked Sier's halfhearted allegiance. "He has made a treaty with Spiritus to keep the Metasymbols separated. He would rely on the FINISHER to dole out the meaning of the prophecy rather than discover it for himself."

Sneering, he continued, "Your father would force Spatium to beg for paltry scraps like a cheap fortune-teller instead of leading like a divine warrior-king!"

That much made sense to Sier. Why be enslaved by some cryptic book that no one understood anymore? Why didn't Caasi and the others rise up and lead Spatium with their own eyes and ears, instead of waiting around like cowards for marching orders that never came?

"Possess and unite the metasymbols and you will be much more than Time-Ruler, if you can even conceive of such power!" the stranger said. The room grew deafeningly silent. The stranger lowered his voice to deliver his next words.

"Yes, you will reign as Time-Ruler, personifying time and controlling all of Spatium, but you will also rule over all of the FINISHER's creation and be the embodiment of enough power to rival the FINISHER himself!"

Sier again shrank back. He could not bring himself to embrace outright rebellion against the FINISHER. He tried to close his mind, to somehow ignore the stranger's taunts.

"A final thought—" the creature paused. "You will also be able to wed whomever you wish, with or without your father's blessing."

"Get out of here!" Sier shouted.

Before the words were completely out of his mouth Sier was released. His body dropped to the floor in a crumpled heap.

The mysterious being disappeared.

∞

"In my opinion, none of the cute ones are smart anyway," Serena said. She sat cross-legged on Hittitaes' bed.

"I don't know how true that is! Amo's cute in his own way," Hittitaes countered from a cushiony chair.

The scent of flowers wafted in through the windows that lined the walls of her palatial bedroom.

"I wonder if you say that because Amo is Sier's brother!" Serena teased.

"Well, I guess, if that's what you like!" Melanie lay sprawled across the floor, flipping through a book. She and Serena had come home with Hittitaes after the Dimensional Games.

"I saw Amo talking to you at the tournament," Serena said. She and Melanie giggled. "He wasn't very suave!"

"Yeah, I mean, come on! Amo is not your type at all," Melanie said.

"I know that," said Hittitaes. "But admit it, he is attractive. Of course, he's no Sier!" She twirled her hair around a finger and let her eyes go dreamy. "But then who is? Besides, I'd be a fool to give Amo a second thought when Sier is chasing!" She sashayed across the room, tossing her hair.

"Why not have a little fun with both?" Serena leaned forward on the bed, a mischievous glint in her eye.

Hittitaes and Melanie turned toward her, eyebrows raised.

"Think about it," Serena continued, "a glance or two in Amo's direction will certainly test Sier's resolve to have you for his own!"

"Now that you mention it," Melanie chimed in, "why should Sier consider you as easily won as the Dimensional Games?"

"Hmm, you may have a point," replied Hittitaes.

Multidimensional Mysteries

CHAPTER 15

Amo stood watching, just outside his father's study. He could see Caasi kneeling, head bent, his back to the open door. Amo imagined his father as he had often seen him, eyes closed, lips fervently moving in silent prayer to the FINISHER.

"Come in, Amo." Caasi remained on his knees and continued, "Why are you watching me? What do you seek?"

"Nothing, Father," Amo faltered, surprised his father was even aware of his presence. He wondered how long Caasi had known he was standing there, allowing him to witness a private moment of devotion and worship.

"You're not speaking the truth, my son." Caasi rose and turned to face Amo.

"I was sure you didn't notice me."

"That is never the case. I'm always conscious of you."

Amo didn't try to hide the doubt that shadowed his face. He cleared his throat and studied the floor. "Sier is at the heart of your attention."

"You're both my sons."

Amo raised his eyes, wringing his hands and turning his back to Caasi. "Yes, but only one of us will be Time-Ruler, and it isn't me. We both know that's all that matters to anyone."

Hurt flickered behind Caasi's eyes. Though by the time he'd crossed the room to place a hand on Amo's shoulder, it was gone, replaced by a steady, unyielding resolve.

"Amo, we are but characters in the FINISHER's book. We do not choose our roles." His hand rested firmly on Amo's shoulder. "My wonderful son, know this for sure, many are called, but few are chosen. The question is, what will you choose when the time comes?"

Amo turned to reply, but Caasi was gone.

"Father? Father!" Amo whirled around, sweeping the study with his eyes but seeing no sign of Caasi. He raced into the hall and bolted up the stairs to his parents' chambers. Riva stood organizing some books on a large, ornate case in their private sitting room.

Amo, breathless, pelted her with questions as he looked around the room.

"Mother, have you seen Father? Did he just come in here?" Amo asked.

"No, dear, your father is at the Temple," Riva said.

"What? That's impossible! I was just with him in the study. I-I spoke with him." Amo's features were a jumble of confusion.

"Are you feeling all right?" Riva walked over and lifted a hand to Amo's cheek.

"Yes, Mother, I'm fine." He absently brushed her hand away. "I need to find Father."

"Shouldn't you be in class?" Riva asked. Amo nodded, quickly leaving the room as he added, "I have questions for Father. I must go to him at the Hall of Letters!"

∞

Cold beads of sweat formed on Amo's brow as he contemplated crossing the Link. He would make the journey utterly alone, without Caasi, even without Rachel. The thought terrified him, but he pressed on. He longed for the moment when at the center of the turbulence, he would call out to the FINISHER and be carried along, trusting the unseen power to bring him safely the other side.

∞

Amo hurriedly descended the ramp from the Link and sprinted up the road leading to the Hall of Letters. He strode through the swirling mist parting before him, past where he and Rachel had hidden from the temple guards. He barely slowed as he approached the massive face of the gleaming pyramid. As before, the guards stood on either side of the soaring arch that lead to the temple's outer court.

"Greetings! I need to enter the temple to speak with my father, Caasi," he blurted, scarcely stopping for a reply before catching sight of Counselor Spiritus in the courtyard. Amo rushed toward him.

"Amo, what are you doing here? Is something wrong? Shouldn't you be in class?"

"Yes, Counselor, I mean, no, sir. I just need to see my father."

"Is there an emergency at home?" Spiritus asked, his brow wrinkling with concern as he noted the anxious look on Amo's face.

"No sir, it's nothing like that," Amo said.

Spiritus let go a sigh of relief. "Good! Unfortunately you won't find your father here. He's already left." He put a hand on Amo's shoulder, steering him back toward the grand arch. "If this is not an emergency I strongly suggest you head to class. And don't worry, I won't tell your father about you being here instead of in physics lecture."

∞

"Ok, settle down everyone." The whirling form of Instructor Em Sartor materialized in the center of a circular lectern. The essence of the Instructor was pure energy, revolving at such a high rate of speed that every point in his body appeared to face outward simultaneously. The effect was that everyone in the room experienced a frontal view of the professor from every angle. Students ceased mingling and chatting; they settled into seats framing the circular lecture hall.

"I have a little surprise for you," the instructor continued, tapping a sheaf of papers on the lectern. "I would like each of you to come forward and give a brief overview of the key tenets of multi-dimensional physics." The class let out a collective groan. "I'm anticipating extremely thoughtful insight on the topic."

A door near the bottom of the classroom swung open and Amo hurried inside, heading for the nearest unoccupied seat. He stumbled and almost fell, tripped up by Tilac's foot surreptitiously stuck out as he passed. A wave of snickers floated upward through the domed hall as Amo regained his composure and took a seat.

"Amo! So glad you could join us," the dervish-like instructor remarked.

"Sorry, sir. I got caught up. It won't happen again."

"He must be the clumsy son of Caasi," jeered a voice from among the other students.

"Well, it's clear he's not the Time-Ruler." The class erupted with laughter.

"Okay, settle down. That's enough!" Instructor Em Sartor tapped his papers against the podium again and cast a penetrating glance at Tilac. "Here's an opportunity to use your feet constructively, master Tilac. Stand and deliver your insights with regard to multi-dimensional physics."

Tilac's seat glowed white, pinpointing his location in the class. He stood for what seemed to him an eternity, unprepared to answer and unsteady in the whirling presence of Instructor Em Sartor.

Sier's hand shot up and was acknowledged by the Instructor. The white light shifted instantly from Tilac to where Sier was already rising from his seat.

"Sir, with all due respect I would like to object to the question being posed on the grounds that no one in the class feels sufficiently prepared in the subject matter. A unanimous vote from the class in favor of suspending the question would justifiably override your instruction."

Murmurs of assent rippled through the hall.

"You are apparently learning to apply the Spatian rule of law opportunistically as you prepare to rule over its citizens." Instructor Em Sartor looked pointedly at Sier. "Your objection is duly noted in the class record. Students, prepare to cast your votes."

Amo raised his hand and addressed the Instructor.

"Yes, Amo?"

"Sir, I vote against tabling the question and request permission to respond."

Tilac whispered, "Flatterer!"

Sier cast a withering sidelong glance at his brother and sat down.

"It appears the vote will not be unanimous in favor of withdrawing the assignment. You may proceed," said Em Sartor.

The white light left Sier's seat and illuminated Amo's.

Amo stood and began speaking. "A single dimension can be defined as a set of unique points in real or abstract space sufficient to determine each element of a system of mathematical entities... the physics of multiple dimensions requires the extrapolation of this concept, possibly to the nth degree..."

Deceptive Invitation

CHAPTER 16

"What's up with your little brother making us look like idiots?" Sier and Tilac had left the physics lecture and were walking across campus.

"No disrespect to you, but Amo should learn to keep his mouth shut instead of making extra work for the rest of us!" Tilac said.

"He needs to be taught a lesson," Sier agreed.

"What do you have in mind?" Tilac grinned.

"Nothing major, just a reminder to stay in his place," Sier said.

∞

Amo and Rachel were walking their usual route home after school.

"You were really great in physics class, although you made the rest of us look kind of stupid!" Rachel said, laughing.

"Well, I wasn't trying to make anyone look bad," Amo said, laughing in return. "I just knew the material, and wanted to share it. Plus, I need the extra credit. I've been slacking lately." He hefted his satchel onto his shoulder. "It had nothing to do with anyone else."

"I'm not sure the rest of the class took it that way," Rachel said.

"Who cares how they took it?" Amo said. "Besides, they're all Sier's lackeys—except you, of course," he added, hastily.

Rachel giggled. "Thanks for not lumping me in with the minions!" she said.

Hittitaes, Serena and Melanie caught up with them, interrupting the conversation. Hittitaes ignored Rachel and slipped an arm around Amo. "Hi!" she said, flashing a radiant smile. "I would love it if you'd escort me to the Unveiling."

"What?" Amo said. "Oh! Uh, yes, of course! It would be my privilege." Amo's voice was a choked whisper. His face turned the crimson of a fireflower in full bloom.

The Unveiling was the first of the many rites of passage that ushered Spatians from one phase of life and responsibility to the next. The ceremonial ritual would elevate them to the ranks of mature citizenship. From then on each Spatian was empowered to choose a mate and to enter into a profession for the benefit of all Spatium. To attend with Hittitaes would only heighten the honor.

"Thank you for your grace," Hittitaes said. She used the formal response.

Amo stared open mouthed as Hittitaes strolled away without so much as a glance in Rachel's direction, Serena and Melanie in tow.

"What was that about?" Rachel huffed, obviously annoyed.

"I'm not sure. Maybe she's attracted to multidimensional physics geeks! Or she could just realize that I'm not a poser, like my brother."

"Yeah, or maybe you're out of your mind not to see she's playing some kind of game with you," Rachel said.

"Are you trying to say that someone like that couldn't be attracted to me?" Amo asked.

Rachel rolled her eyes, but continued patiently. "No, I'm not saying that at all," she said. "I just think it's a little strange that at the

Dimensional Games she's passionately kissing your brother in front of a huge crowd, but now she's asking you to the Unveiling."

Rachel stood, looking up at him. "That doesn't sound just a little bit strange to you?" she asked.

Amo shifted his weight and started to reply.

"Oh, no. What do they want?" Rachel asked. She could see Sier's cronies Tilac, Raze and Dub swaggering in their direction.

Amo turned to face them. Tilac was nearly as tall as Sier, and Amo had to tilt his head slightly to look into his eyes.

"How 'bout some company to liven up your walk home?" Tilac jeered.

"How about I break your legs and drag you to your mother's doorstep?" Rachel glared, squaring off in front of Raze.

"I'd love for you to try!" His lips pealed back in a salacious grin.

"Our clash isn't with you, little girl, so keep quiet." Tilac stepped between Raze and Rachel, shoving her aside.

Amo made a move for Tilac and was grabbed from behind, then wrapped up in a full nelson by Dub. He struggled to no avail against Dub's considerable heft.

Raze reared back and punched him hard in the stomach. Amo doubled over but Dub yanked him upright. His shoulders were instantly on fire. They felt like they would come out of their sockets. His head jerked left as Tilac belted him across the mouth and leaned in, his face inches away. Amo licked his split lip, tasting his own blood.

"What's with showing us up like that? Your little physics rant is gonna cost you!" Tilac stepped back and Raze slammed a fist into Amo's gut. Rachel pounced on him, but he easily held her at arm's length.

"I don't care what you think you have to prove," Tilac sneered, "you're not gonna make us look like idiots to do it!"

"Too late!" Rachel screamed, struggling to push past Raze's stiff arm.

"I don't know what you're talking about," Amo wheezed. His peripheral vision was shrinking and a thousand tiny sparks like glitter floated in front of his eyes. He was going to black out.

"Let's get out of here. I think he gets the message." Tilac walked away as Dub released Amo, dropping him to his knees.

Amo gulped in air as mind numbing pain seared through his shoulders.

Rachel was on her knees beside him, tears streaking her face. "Are you ok?" she sobbed.

He nodded slowly, clearing his head and gingerly stretching his shoulders down and forward. Rachel gently ran her hand through his hair.

"Yea I'm fine. Just a little beat up." He smiled wanly. "I think my pride hurts most, but I'll survive."

"Yeah." Rachel sniffed. "Those imbeciles were on a mission! Will you get beat up whenever you do something Sier doesn't like?"

She helped Amo slowly to his feet and picked up his books. "I can't believe your brother would sick those morons on you! They're too dumb to be offended on their own."

Amo rubbed his aching shoulders and took his book sack from Rachel. A fresh shard of pain lanced his shoulder, but he grimaced and hefted the pack anyway.

They walked along in silence for a while, each lost in their own thoughts. Rachel wondered how she could ever go through with her vow to wed Sier; the self-serving brute! She stole a glance at Amo and her heart melted. She longed to tend to his bruises, to hold him close, to tell him the truth.

Amo inhaled deeply, brooding over his brother's treachery. His mood darkened like a storm slowly gathering strength in his mind. Did Sier mean to crush him in everything? Let him try! Amo vowed he would rather fall off the Link than live under Sier's tyranny.

When they reached the path leading to Rachel's house they stopped to say their goodbyes.

Amo lowered his books to the ground, thankful to let the throbbing ache in his shoulders distract him for a moment.

Rachel reached up to hug him, careful not to cause more pain. He looked down and smiled into her tear-stained face.

"At least one good thing came out of this..." Amo remembered, his eyes slowly brightening.

"What could that possibly be?" Rachel's heart raced. She stood before Amo breathless, hoping he might share her feelings for him.

"I still get to take Hittitaes to the Unveiling!"

Twin bolts of lightning electrified his shoulders as Rachel punched Amo squarely in the chest. He just caught a glimpse of the hurt and anger in her eyes before she ran sobbing up the path to her house.

"What the—?" He stood dazed for a moment, feeling confused and betrayed, first by his brother, and now by his friend.

Fragile Alliances

CHAPTER 17

"Counselor Spiritus has arrived, dear." Riva opened the door to Caasi's study and stuck her head inside.

"Thank you," Caasi said. "Please send the Counselor in."

"Welcome, friend!" Caasi greeted Counselor Spiritus and embraced him. He motioned toward one of two comfortable chairs flanking a low table. "I'm glad you've come. Please, sit down."

Riva discreetly entered with a tray of warm drinks and light refreshments. She set it on the table and smiled, nodding briefly at Caasi. She gave Spiritus' shoulder a gentle squeeze. She exited the study and closed the door quietly behind her, leaving them alone to talk.

"So, have you spoken with Rachel?" Caasi poured steaming mugs for both of them as Spiritus helped himself to some fruit.

"I have, though she was less than enthusiastic about the arrangement." Spiritus wrinkled his brow as he took a sip from his mug. "Rachel dances to a beat all her own," he sighed. "She resents having this important part of her life governed. She is determined to chart her own course." He paused, noticing Caasi leaning forward in his chair, a worried look shadowing his face.

Spiritus spread his hands resignedly. "Nevertheless, Rachel will honor the commitment I have made in order to preserve the realm."

"Indeed, Caduceus grows bolder at each reading of the Book of Fabula and Syuzhet," Caasi nodded. "Our united effort will be required to quash his hints at rebellion."

"And what of Sier? Is he firmly committed to cementing the alliance by marrying my daughter?" Spiritus posed the question directly. He hoped Sier was devoted to their cause. That would quiet his misgivings about consigning Rachel to such an arranged marriage.

Caasi was silent for a long moment. "Sier will make an exceptional warrior-king. I believe his power is even now unparalleled; he will reign unequaled as Time-Ruler." He locked eyes with his friend and continued, "As a husband to Rachel, however..."

Spiritus nodded, his anxiety mounting.

Caasi read the growing concern in his friend's face and was helpless to assuage his doubts. He pressed on, knowing that to withhold his suspicions would ruin their friendship, and perhaps topple the alliance so vital to keeping Caduceus in check and maintaining Spatium's loyalty to the FINISHER. "I believe Sier has developed a fondness for Caduceus' daughter, Hittitaes," he announced. "It is being said that at the Dimensional Games, he scarcely veiled his intent to have her as his wife."

Spiritus stood and walked toward the large windows framing a breathtaking view of Spatium and the mountains in the distance. He slowly inhaled the spicy scent of a profusion of flowers blanketing the hillside and exhaled even more slowly.

"Hittitaes is a beautiful woman," he said. "Still, a marriage between Sier and her would all but cede the power of Time-Ruler to Caduceus."

Caasi, who had remained seated, now rose to face his friend. "To allow it would bring desecration to Spatium."

Spiritus nodded.

"It is settled, then," Caasi agreed. "We will announce the covenant at the Unveiling."

∞

"What happened to your face?" Riva leaned in toward Amo, inspecting an ugly cut and bruise.

"It's nothing, Mom. I cut myself at the Axle." He winced as Riva touched his swollen lower lip.

"That looks serious," she said, looking concerned. "Have you been in a fight?"

"No, not at all. It was just a game. Things got a little rough."

"If you were in a fight, where was Sier? He should've stood up for you!" She didn't wait for an answer but instead hurried off toward the kitchen for some herbs. "Let me go grab something to put on that."

"Mom, would he protect me?" Amo asked.

Riva halted and turned toward him. "Who?"

"Sier. Do you think he would protect me?"

"Of course, he would! He's your brother." She smiled and headed for the kitchen.

Amo nodded. He said nothing as his mother left.

∞

Amo stood in the backyard, wondering how to confront Sier's

duplicity. The gentle breeze blowing through the garden picked up strength.

Counselor Spiritus had left Caasi's study and was making his way through the garden at the back of the house when he spotted Amo standing alone. His face was drawn taut, his lips pressed in a thin angry line.

As the Counselor watched, the sky grew overcast, and the once gentle breeze grew steadily stronger until it howled through the garden, uprooting plants and overturning everything in its path. Spiritus made his way toward the still figure of Amo, whose growing rage manifested in the intensifying storm. Lightning flashed, highlighting the house and shrubs in stark relief.

"Amo!" Spiritus shouted.

Amo thought of Sier sending his underlings to teach him a lesson. He let the rage come, vaguely aware that his anger was erupting in a storm that threatened to decimate the garden where he stood. The air around him was electrified. He could barely contain the surge of raw power rising within him. He struggled to subdue the energy. Somehow, he knew it could rip all of Spatium apart if he failed to reign it in.

"Amo!" Spiritus shouted, again.

He heard a strong voice calling his name over the noise of the storm. He turned to find Counselor Spiritus calling out to him. The sound of the Counselor's voice calmed him, and by degrees, the storm ceased. Everything suddenly restored to order. The warm, bright light from the expanse returned, and the spicy, refreshing scent of flowers again filled his mother's garden.

"That was pretty impressive," the Counselor said, crossing the garden and closing the distance between them.

"Thank you, Counselor. I think..." Amo was uncertain what to make of his newfound power.

"It appears you have tremendous talent," Counselor Spiritus said. "I would like to teach you to control your power, to harness it to your will."

"Wouldn't that interfere with your work with Sier?" Amo looked pointedly at Counselor Spiritus. "I mean no disrespect, Counselor, but Sier is to be Time-Ruler."

"Nonetheless, power such as you display should not go undisciplined," the Counselor replied. He raised his eyes to a point far off in the distance above Amo's head. "Many things yet remain to be deciphered, including the role you are to play under your brother's reign." He walked out of the garden as Amo stared after him. "I will be in touch," he said.

Amo thought maybe things were turning in his favor. He would escort the most beautiful girl in Spatium to the Unveiling, and the noble Counselor Spiritus had agreed to mentor him, even if to serve under Sier.

Seeing the Counselor brought Rachel to mind. Amo decided he needed to make amends and return to the Hall of Letters. He hoped the Book of Fabula and Syuzhet would shed some light on the unfolding events.

Fabula and Syuzhet

CHAPTER 18

The sound of another clink against the window made Rachel get up from her chair to investigate.

"Rachel! Rachel!" Amo called to her. His voice carried up to her second-story window.

"What are you doing here?" Rachel opened the window and peered out. Amo stood below, tilting his head and looking up at her.

"Look, I'm sorry for whatever I did to upset you," he said. "Please come down. I need to talk to you, right away!"

"Whatever you did to upset me?" Rachel asked. "That's a lame apology, even for you!"

"You know me well enough to know that if I said it, I meant it," Amo said, "no matter how lame it sounded. If you don't come down here, I'll come up and get you, myself!"

Rachel half-heartedly accepted Amo's apology. They were friends. He probably was clueless that she wanted to be more than that. Besides, she had vowed to leave those feelings alone.

"Short of breaking into our house and enraging my father, just how will you do that?" Rachel taunted, shrugging her shoulders. She'd decided to forgive Amo, but she was content to let him try to make good on his threat to take her from the window.

"Like this!" Amo put his hand forward and pushed down against an invisible force that sent him rocketing skyward. His other arm and legs flailing, he adjusted the pressure of his hand and struggled to gain control. Just beneath Rachel's window, he extended his left hand up and out to her.

"Come on, give me your hand," he said. "I'm not very good at this yet."

Rachel's mouth hung open, her eyes wide. "How are you—?"

"Don't try to figure it out now, Rachel! Come on, give me your hand," Amo insisted. "Don't look down. Keep your eyes on me."

Rachel climbed through the open window and sat on the ledge. She reached out and, grasping Amo's hand, stepped gingerly out into thin air. Their eyes met, and the air rippled beneath them.

"Remember, don't look down," Amo said. He gathered Rachel in his arms and slowly began their descent. His feet hit the ground first. His knees buckled, causing the two of them to land in a heap.

"Are you okay?" Amo asked. He lifted Rachel from his chest.

"Fine," Rachel said. "Thanks for softening my landing." She stood and brushed herself off.

"Great, now how about returning the favor?" Amo asked.

"Don't you have any pride?" Rachel asked. "I just forgave you for whatever, you crash land me from the second floor, and now you're already asking me for—what?"

"I need to return to the Hall of Letters," Amo said. "I'll go alone, but I'd rather have you with me."

∞

"They're not going to fall for the same trick," Amo said. He and Rachel stood looking at the guards of the Protectorate in the distance. "We need to find another way in."

"I'm fresh out of ideas," Rachel smirked.

"Me, too." Amo smiled.

"How did you do that, back at my window?" Rachel eyed him quizzically. "What's going on with you?"

"I'm learning." Amo said. He knelt and spread his hands on the ground. "That gives me an idea."

"What are you doing?" Rachel asked.

"Being creative," Amo said. "If I can hide us, can you lead us past the guards and into the courtyard?" he asked.

"I don't need eyes to see," Rachel said.

Rachel was the daughter of Counselor Spiritus, and she had inherited his gift of spiritual sight. She stood beside Amo and watched as he pressed his palms against the soft ground. His hands disappeared beneath the mist nearly up to his elbows.

The mist rose and grew thicker until it became a dense fog enveloping the area where they hid. It thickened to the high arch where the guards stood.

"You ready?" Rachel asked. Her disembodied voice came from just in front of Amo. In the whiteness of the fog, she was invisible. Amo felt her hands grasp his and place them on her shoulders.

"Yes. Let's go," he said. Following Rachel's lead, Amo slowed his breathing and focussed, moving in unison with her every step.

With her eyes shut and her mind open, Rachel took in their surroundings. She could see as clearly as though there were no fog at all. She led them the remaining distance to the Hall of Letters, slowing her pace so that Amo could follow without tripping, his hands firmly on her shoulders.

As they approached the arch, she heard the guards discussing the sudden fog storm without concern, confident it would dissipate soon. She and Amo walked past them undetected and into the temple courtyard.

Once they were inside, Rachel opened her eyes and turned to face Amo. He took her hand and hurried them toward the massive doors that led to the outer sanctuary. They passed the conference rooms, then hurried through the hollow arch full of twisted, silvery trees. Light poured in from the crystal pinnacle and glinted off the white-gold walls.

Seeing no one, they entered the Great Hall. They crossed to the emerald table that glowed softly in the center of the room. Just beyond it, they could see the sacred book of Fabula and Syuzhet where it lay unopened atop its pedestal.

Amo and Rachel cautiously approached the pedestal, eyes fastened on the shimmering book. As they reached it, the book began to vibrate. It glowed brightly, then flung open. Its mirrored contents fluttered in a torrent of flipping pages.

Suddenly, the activity stopped, and the book lay open, its energy spent. Amo and Rachel leaned closer. They gasped at their reflection on the open pages of the book. Their images liquified, replaced by symbols which slowly appeared, forming words above the book's shimmering surface.

"What does it mean?" Rachel whispered.

"I'm not sure," Amo said.

They jumped at the sound of voices coming from just beyond the silvery trees. There was nowhere to hide. They'd surely be seen before they could reach the doors at the rear of the hall.

Amo stepped close to Rachel. He wrapped his arms around her and sent them both hurtling upward, toward the pyramid's crystal apex.

Sier, Tilac, and Raze rushed into the Great Hall of the temple and fanned out over the room.

"There's nothing here," Tilac said.

"We'll check the other rooms—" Sier halted in mid-stride, his attention focused on the Book of Fabula and Syuzhet.

"Someone's been in here," he said. He spun around, searching the room. He moved backward, toward the sacred book.

"I thought you said the Hall of Letters would be empty," Tilac said, nervously. He and Raze inched closer to Sier.

"It is, but look," Sier said. "Someone has opened the Book of Fabula and Syuzhet. My father says it's always closed after the reading. It's open now, which means someone has just been reading it."

Rachel held her breath. She squeezed her eyes shut so tight, she thought her eyeballs would burst.

Amo watched as Sier scanned the Great Hall again, determined to discover whoever had just been reading the book. He and Rachel hung motionless, suspended high in the air above the chamber.

Sier leaned over the book, peering into its pages. His face leaped into view above the mirrored sheets along with a string of cryptic symbols.

"What does it mean?" Tilac breathed over Sier's shoulder.

"I don't know," Sier replied. "But someone has been here reading the Book of Fabula and Syuzhet—"

"Whoever was in here has already left," Raze said. He stood, remaining some distance from the pedestal.

"Yes, it would seem so," Sier said. He didn't sound convinced.

"Let's just find the Meta symbols and get out of here!" Raze said, eyeing the door. He was eager to be far from this place.

Sier nodded as he, Tilac, and Raze exited the room.

Amo and Rachel remained where they were until they no longer heard the sounds of Sier and the others moving about.

"What were they looking for?" Rachel asked.

Amo lowered them both to the floor. "I have no clue," he said.

"Is Sier trying to study the prophecy, too?" Rachel asked.

"I don't think so," Amo said, "but they were definitely looking for something." His eyes darted about the room.

Rachel nodded. "I'm just glad they didn't find us," she said.

"Yeah, that was a close call," Amo said.

Rachel was already heading for the doors. "Let's get out of here, before something else crazy happens," she called over her shoulder.

Amo followed, stopping short in front of the pedestal. "This time, I'll remember to close the book of Fabula and Syuzhet."

They Should Be Worried

CHAPTER 19

Rachel and Amo again crossed the Link. Together, they sought the presence of the FINISHER in the storm and were safely brought to the other side. The bond of their friendship deepened with the mystical journey. They descended the ramp and crossed the flatland. Soon they entered a small wood, the other side of which led to the gently sloping hillsides near their homes.

"I'm not sure how I would have explained being in the temple to my brother," Amo said. "And if my father found out he would have dispatched me for sure!" He was only half-joking.

∞

Sier motioned for Tilac and Raze to be quiet, as they sat in a circle a little way in from the path that leads through the woods. Various items they had stolen from the Hall of Letters lay spread out between them.

"Shhh!" Sier held a finger to his lips, cocked his head and listened. He was sure he heard voices in the woods toward the path.

∞

"What do you think Sier was looking for in the Hall of Letters?" Rachel asked. She and Amo started along the meandering path through the woods.

"I don't know," Amo said. "It's strange that he'd be there, especially with Tilac and Raze."

"What did they mean by 'Meta symbols?'" Rachel asked.

"You heard that, too?" Amo asked. "I don't have a clue what they are, but Sier and the others seemed to think they're somewhere in the temple."

∞

Sier, Tilac, and Raze had quietly gathered up the articles from the temple and hid alongside the path. They watched as Amo and Rachel walked along between the trees. The wood was shrouded in a deepening mist; the canopy of leaves and branches cast shadows on the ground below. Crouching out of sight, Sier and the others silently crept to within earshot.

"How about we have some fun?" Sier whispered, grinning at Tilac and Raze in the deepening gloom. They grinned back, heads bobbing in demented unison. "Follow my lead."

∞

"...get home so our parents won't worry." The tail end of Amo's comment floated through the trees.

Sier heard his brother's words as he knelt in the mist at the base of a tree just beyond the path.

"Maybe they should be worried…"

An eery, disembodied voice seemed to come from deep in the woods, halting Amo and Rachel in their tracks.

"Did you say that?" Amo asked Rachel, hoping the voice he'd heard had been hers, but knowing it hadn't.

"No." Rachel's voice trembled slightly, but she cleared her throat and continued, "Probably just the—"

"*They should be worried! They should be worried!*" The words echoed around them in the woods. The sound seemed to come from everywhere at once.

"Let's get out of here!" Amo grabbed Rachel's hand. They took off running along the path.

Tilac and Raze picked up the taunt. Taking turns with Sier, they howled and shrieked the ominous words as they ran alongside the path, through the wood.

Raze doubled back, falling in behind Amo and Rachel. He kept out of sight among the trees.

Amo tried to look past the treeline, but he couldn't see anything. Low hanging branches crowded the path, blocking his view. He didn't dare stop running before they reached the open field. There, he could turn and position himself to fight between Rachel and whatever might follow them out of the wood.

"*They should be worried!*" The words rang out from in front and behind them, growing louder and more maniacal, even as they ran, faster and faster along the twisting path. Soon the end of the trees was in sight. Amo and Rachel noticed the wood thinning at the same time. They picked up speed, bolting for the grassy hillside.

Sier hung back as Amo and Rachel escaped the wood and shot out into the clearing. Tilac and Raze caught up to him and followed suit. The three of them struggled to catch their breath and stifle their laughter.

Amo and Rachel continued running until they were well clear of the trees. Amo stopped and turned to face the wood.

"What are you doing?" Rachel demanded. She had run a few paces past Amo after he'd pulled up short. Breathless, she turned, and half-shouted, half croaked the question.

"Keep running, Rachel! I can't risk whatever that was catching us by surprise in the open!" He turned to reassure her. "I'll be right ba—"

The piercing sound of Rachel's scream curdled Amo's blood in his veins.

A large, hulking figure sauntered toward them from within the fog at the edge of the woods. One, then another dark form took shape behind the first, falling into step and steadily gaining ground.

∞

"Go, Rachel!" Amo readied himself to fight. His heart pounded in his chest, but his mind seemed suddenly to focus. He determined to unleash a powerful burst of energy against whatever was coming. He stretched his hands out in front of him and felt the intensity of the fireball build.

He targeted the first advancing figure, and as he prepared to let fly, the familiar face of his brother came into view. Sier emerged from the fog.

"Sier! What are you doing?" Amo yelled.

"I should ask you the same question, brother," Sier said. His voice was steady.

"We were walking in the wood," Amo said as Rachel returned to stand beside him. He stepped protectively in front of her.

Tilac and Raze gathered behind Sier.

"Liar!" Sier spat.

"If you know I'm lying, then you already know where I was." Amo took a threatening step toward Sier. "What were you looking for in the Hall of Letters?"

"That's none of your concern!" Sier glowered. "If you know what's good for you, you'll forget I was there!"

"What are you trying to hide?" Rachel stepped out from behind Amo.

"Let's just say there'd be trouble for all of us if our visit to the temple were discovered." Sier cast an insinuating glance at Amo. "But I'm telling you, it could be much worse for you—"

Sier suddenly stretched his hand forward and enveloped Rachel in a dazzling sphere of blue-white light. Instantly her body began to age rapidly, before their eyes.

"*No!*" Amo charged toward Sier, but Tilac and Raze anticipated him. They caught him just short of where Sier stood. They pinned his arms behind his back.

"Relax, little brother! She'll be fine, except for the fall," Sier sneered. Raising the sphere and Rachel above his head, he restored her body and dropped it to the ground.

"Keep your mouth shut, or I'll do worse," Sier threatened. He motioned for Tilac and Raze to let Amo loose and walked away.

Amo glared after his brother. He had never seen anything like what Sier had done to Rachel. Of course, Sier would manifest abilities even more significant than his own burgeoning ones. Sier would be Time-Ruler. Perhaps working with Spiritus would shed some light on his power.

Amo pushed his racing thoughts aside. He rushed over to where Rachel's crumpled figure lay on the ground.

"Rachel, Rachel? Are you okay?" he asked, kneeling beside her.

"I think so," Rachel said. I feel like I fell off a cliff! I was watching you and Sier arguing, and now, here I am. How did I...?" She looked around, bewildered.

"It's a long story," Amo said, suddenly wanting to take Rachel and be gone from the spot. "Come on, let me help you up." He lifted her gently to her feet. She stood shakily, and he put an arm around her to steady her. "Let's get you back. No need to worry your father."

Amo held Rachel close, and she leaned into him as they walked home.

∞

"How will we know if any of this stuff is what we're looking for?"

Sier, Tilac, and Raze huddled in the corner of Sier's room. They eyed the articles they'd stolen from the Hall of Letters.

Tilac had asked the question, doubtful they'd be able to identify the mysterious symbols Sier was suddenly so eager to find.

"I'm not sure it'll be something that stands out..." Sier continued rifling through the items. He picked up one after another for closer examination. "This is useless! I'm not even sure what the symbols look like!" he said.

"If only we could see one," offered Raze, "maybe it wouldn't be so hard to find the others."

Sier paused, considering the words he'd heard from the mysterious white entity. Why hadn't he thought of it before! Spiritus possessed one of the meta symbols. Raze was onto something—if Sier could see it for himself, he was confident it would make finding the others much easier.

"I think I can do exactly that," Sier murmured aloud.

Tilac and Raze were instantly at attention.

"But I'll need to do it alone," Sier said, rising to leave the room.

Face to Face

CHAPTER 20

"I'm just no good at this!" Sier had failed repeatedly in his attempts to embrace and manipulate a concept foreign to him.

"You're correct, you are no good at this! You *are* this!" Counselor Spiritus chided. "Concentrate! You are not creating time. You must locate time where it is and grasp it; seize it and internalize it! Make it your attribute!"

Sier closed his eyes and focussed on the idea that the events of existence could be funneled single file through a unique point called "now." He reached out with his thoughts and attempted to order all that there was around that point. His very being violently rejected the idea that some events were "past;" they had moved through the point of "now," while others waiting beyond that point were "future." The air around the pupil and student grew heavy with Sier's effort. Arcs of electrical energy exploded around them. All of existence recoiled at being forced into the line called "time."

"Much better!" said Spiritus.

Sier didn't think so.

"Remember, time is the property of the FINISHER, Spiritus said. "Rely on him to direct your interaction with it. You must proceed calmly. Your frustration will only hinder the learning process."

Spiritus appeared thoughtful for a moment. "Perhaps you'll have more success if we reduce the components to familiar elements, allowing you to manipulate events on a smaller scale."

Spiritus led Sier to a bank of transparent half-cylinders lining the wall. A hissing sound escaped as the door nearest them swung open. The chamber was just wide enough for Sier to step inside.

∞

"This kind of training is my brother's domain, not mine!" Amo stood, sweating and breathless, in the center of the Axle.

"You are indeed a son of Caasi, and ability such as yours must not go undisciplined," Counselor Spiritus reminded him. "You are not capable of controlling this power on your own." He waited until Amo nodded his head in agreement, then he said, "We also need to see where your unique strengths lie."

Counselor Spiritus led Amo to the bank of simulation chambers. "Your brother has honed his powers tremendously using the simulator." He opened one of the transparent half-cylinders and instructed Amo to step inside. "I expect it may help you as well."

∞

The simulated sky glowed burnt orange and red, with lavender and blue streaks stretching from one horizon to the other. Sweat drenched his body as Amo raced over the jagged terrain. The sound of his own heart pounded, and the muscles of his legs strained with the effort to stay ahead.

A monster born of his fears bore down on him steadily. The blast of a white-hot sphere of pure energy whizzed past, singeing the hairs on his neck. He ran on, desperate for the safety of his mother and home. He'd been in this situation before. Amo swiveled his head around to look back. Heart racing, he ducked low and just dodged a blow that he was sure would have decapitated him.

∞

Spiritus watched Amo struggle in the grip of a battle created especially for him by the simulator. He continued to monitor various streams of output. Suddenly his eyes widened in disbelief. His mouth hung open, his mind unable to comprehend the measurements being recorded by the instruments. He re-calibrated the probes and stared in alarm as the indicators flew off the chart.

∞

In the split second, it had taken to glance behind him, Amo recognized the monster hunting him and became enraged. Counselor Spiritus had been right about the simulator. It distilled his greatest fears down to a single, horrifyingly accurate manifestation that he could not outrun. The realization brought a fresh surge of anger. He turned to fight, catching the wildly lurching beast off guard. He stretched himself long and low along the ground, extending his legs across the monster's path. In an instant, it was flying through the air, tripped up by Amo's stiffened legs banging against its own.

Instinctively, Amo hurled his sphere of white-hot light in the monster's direction, capturing it in a bubble of pure energy. He concentrated, all at once, he understood Spiritus' instruction. He could see it—time, a million instances flowing single file through one blindingly bright point, one "now." He experienced each one in succession; it was like nothing he had ever known. The fragmentation of existence was excruciating, almost more than he could bear.

He turned his attention to the monster in the sphere. His brother's face stared back at him.

∞

Counselor Spiritus watched as Amo strode angrily from the Axle's cavernous training room.

The Counselor was certain Amo had manipulated the simulator's inputs. There was no other explanation for the incredible, off the scale measurements it had recorded. Spiritus confronted Amo when he emerged from the battle sequence.

The data had been corrupted. Counselor Spiritus was convinced of it. Not even Sier had generated such phenomenal power as to nearly overwhelm the simulator.

Of course, Amo had denied any misconduct. Counselor Spiritus clenched his fists subconsciously, the whitened knuckles of his hands protruding through the skin.

Perhaps Amo had deceived the simulator in some way, he thought. It had been a mistake to encourage him to probe the enigma of time. Had his darkest traits been amplified by the exposure? The burden of living in Sier's shadow was perhaps too much for Amo to bear.

Spiritus massaged his temples as though trying to rub away his troubled thoughts. Even Rachel had come home crying and then there was some incident involving Amo in the woods. He had witnessed the destructive power of Amo's uncontrolled anger in the garden outside the Caasi home.

It was settled then. He had made the right decision to abandon mentoring Amo in light of his duplicity. Sier was the chosen one. The book of Fabula and Syuzhet could not be wrong.

∞

Amo slammed the door as he left the Axle. His thoughts were a million white-hot bombs exploding in his mind. He felt he had barely survived the mind-numbing experience of time in the simulator.

And now, he wondered, *how could Spiritus accuse him of cheating the machine?*

Prelude to The Unveiling

CHAPTER 21

"Look who just walked in." Serena nodded toward the door. Hittitaes shifted in her seat, looking around just as Sier entered The Quest. Seeing her, he made his way through the   crowded club to their table.

"Have you told him you're going to the Unveiling with Amo?" Serena asked, eyes riveted on the approaching Sier.

Hittitaes sighed, returning her attention to Serena and Melanie. "Not yet," she said with a shrug.

"Well, here's your chance," Melanie grinned, blushing as Sier reached their table and sat down next to Hittitaes.

"You look great," Sier said, reaching for Hittitaes' hand on the table. He nodded politely toward the other girls, barely glancing in their direction. "Hi, ladies," he said.

Melanie and Serena murmured greetings.

Sier leaned in close to Hittitaes, "Let me be your escort for the Unveiling," he said.

An uncomfortable silence lingered over the table.

"I'm sorry, Sier, I'm going with someone else," Hittitaes said.

She allowed her glance to slide over the other patrons. She let it rest where Amo and Rachel were talking at another table.

Sier followed her gaze. After a moment, its implication struck him full force. "My brother?" he retorted. "You can't be serious!"

"I'd love for you to be my escort..." Melanie's voice trailed off as Sier left the table. Hittitaes and Serena watched, as Sire marched toward Amo and Rachel.

"You're a fool if you think Hittitaes wants you!" Sier glared across the table at Amo. "Rachel," Sier nodded. He turned and left the club.

"Your brother's right, you know," Rachel said.

"I don't need you siding with him, Rachel." Amo shifted in his seat.

"I'm just saying. You can't keep your eyes off her, but she just sits there like she hardly knows you." Rachel stared daggers at Hittitaes across the room.

"She's just hanging out with her friends. I'm sure things would be different if I went over to her," Amo said.

Rachel rolled her eyes doubtfully.

"Hittitaes and I are going to the Unveiling together whether you and Sier like it or not!" Amo snapped.

"What has gotten into you?" Rachel countered, her voice rising. "You're a fool if you think that shameless poser has real feelings for you!"

Several heads turned in their direction. A few stared open-mouthed at what was turning into a heated exchange.

"That's enough!" Amo snapped.

"I'll tell you what's enough—" Rachel shot back, "Everyone knows she's using you, except you!" Suddenly, she was on her feet, her face flushed with anger. "Have fun looking like an idiot!"

Amo sat staring as Rachel turned and stalked out of The Quest.

"This is ridiculous!" He shoved his chair from the table and pushed through the crowd to where Hittitaes, Serena, and Melanie were sitting.

Absorbed by her confrontation with Amo, Rachel was startled by Sier's approach outside the club.

"Rachel," he said, "I think we need to talk."

∞

"Are you ok, son?" Caasi opened the door to Sier's room and stuck his head in.

"I thought I heard something up here," Caasi continued. "I didn't realize you'd returned."

"I just got here," Sier replied. "I'm fine." He tensed, painfully aware of the bag containing the stolen articles from the Hall of Letters on his bed. He had barely tucked the last of the items away as Caasi had entered his room.

"I've been meaning to talk with you about attending the Unveiling with Rachel."

Sier lifted the bag and pushed it under his bed. Caasi found a chair and sat down.

"I think it would be a demonstration of good faith to Spiritus, as well as a prime opportunity to announce the impending treaty between our houses."

"I agree, father," Sier responded. "I have already presented myself to Rachel as escort to the Unveiling." He stood beside the bed, facing Caasi. "She has accepted."

"That's excellent news," Caasi exclaimed, though his face looked puzzled. "I must admit I'm surprised to hear it. Your mother said she noticed you and Hittitaes, uh, celebrating your victory at the Dimensional Games." He peered closely into his son's face.

Sier maintained a guarded expression.

Caasi continued. "I want to be sure we remain in agreement regarding the treaty and your union with Rachel."

"I will honor your plans," Sier said, flatly "The kiss with Hittitaes was just that—a spontaneous celebration of my success."

"Hmm." Caasi was thoughtful. He sighed heavily. "I know you are making a tremendous sacrifice of your own desires, my son," he said.

∞

"Sier will be escorting Rachel to the dance, after all." Caasi caressed his wife Riva's shoulder absently as he spoke. "Although I'm sure she isn't his first choice, she is his best choice." They sat together on a luxurious sofa in the family room.

"How were you able to convince him to do that?" Riva asked.

"I didn't have to convince him at all. Before I could suggest it, he informed me he'd already asked, and she'd accepted."

Riva frowned, looking doubtful.

"It appears our worries have been for naught," Caasi announced.

"I'm not so sure." Riva twisted a strand of her braided hair between her fingers. "If he wants Hittitaes, he'll have her. He may be telling you only what you want to hear. I saw that kiss at the Games. It looked a lot more than congratulatory."

"I guarantee you; it was exactly that!" Caasi and Riva looked up at the sound of Amo's voice, loud in the quiet of the room.

"Hittitaes will attend the Unveiling with me," he continued, heedlessly interrupting their conversation. "And I assure you, she feels nothing for Sier," he said. He turned and left the room without waiting for a reply.

"What's gotten into him?" Caasi wondered aloud.

"I'm not sure," Riva replied. "Perhaps he cares for Hittitaes more than he's let on."

"He has much to bear," Cassi said. "Amo must serve his brother, and his brother will have his best friend as wife. Amo may well see things as you do, that if Sier wants Hittitaes, he will have her, regardless of Amo's feelings."

Caasi rubbed a hand over his forehead in frustration.

"Are they fated to compete in everything?" he wondered aloud. "Have I encouraged them to be rivals more than brothers?"

Riva gave her husband's thigh a pat. "You are a good father to your sons," she said simply.

Caasi drew his wife close. They held each other in a comfortable embrace, each deep in their own thoughts.

The Giving of the Rings

CHAPTER 22

The people of Spatium gathered in solemn celebration of its most highly esteemed occasion. Colored gems embedded in the walls of the outer court of the Hall of Letters sparkled in the soft light.

Along one side of the chamber, Spatium's progenitors stood under the alcove where Rachel and Amo had hidden from the temple guards. Magnificently attired, they were arranged in an intricate geometric pattern across the floor.

The honorees, equally resplendent in ceremonial garb, mirrored their parents' position under an identical alcove on the opposite side of the courtyard.

The ceremony of the Unveiling initiated rites of passage that paved the way for Spatium's next leaders. The extravagant ritual elevated Spatians to the ranks of mature citizenship. Through the ceremony, they were empowered to choose mates and professions in the service of the FINISHER and for the benefit of all Spatium.

Bells chimed throughout the chamber, signaling the start of the ceremony. The participants emerged from beneath the alcoves and strolled about the temple court. They maintained the elaborate pattern's symmetry until the two groups met in the center of the room. In a spectacular display, they merged to form a single new pattern in front of the massive doors leading to the outer sanctuary.

Each Spatian young lady was led by her parents to her escort, who stood at his place in the pattern, flanked by his parents. All were attired in a brilliant array of sumptuous fabrics. They shimmered under the soft light from the pyramid's crystal apex.

Counselor Spiritus led Rachel to where Caasi, Riva, and Sier waited.

"You're simply breathtaking, my dear," Riva said. She kissed Rachel on both cheeks in ceremonial greeting.

Rachel extended her hand and Caasi brushed his lips against it, offering his compliments as well.

Spiritus, Caasi, and Riva then formed a semi-circle behind Rachel and lowered themselves; Spiritus and Caasi bowing and Riva curtsying elegantly as they presented Rachel to Sier.

She wore a long, full gown of the palest iridescent silk.

The watery sheen of it reflected light in a soft halo around her. Sier had never seen Rachel look so beautiful, and her fiery eyes held the hint of a challenge he had somehow failed to notice. Gone was her characteristic ponytail; instead, the warm brown of her hair was loosely swept atop her head.

Aware that perhaps he had allowed his gaze to linger a little too long, Sier offered his arm, into which Rachel slipped hers. "You look beautiful, Rachel," he whispered against her hair.

"You, too," she quipped. Sier laughed at her comment and whisked her toward the sanctuary doors to await the start of the procession.

Behind them, Caasi and Riva returned to their place as progenitors, where they joined Amo in welcoming Caduceus and Hittitaes.

Amo's breath caught in his throat as Caduceus led his daughter in the ritual pattern toward where he and his parents stood.

Hittitaes' auburn hair cascaded over her shoulders. Soft curls of it framed her face and fell onto her smooth skin. Several strands of delicate, graduated filigree chains encircled her throat, lengthening to disappear beneath the folds of her gown. Its whispery blue silk flowed around her, a living complement to her every move.

Caasi and Riva stepped forward to warmly greet Caduceus and Hittitaes before making the ritual presentation of Hittitaes as a gift to Amo.

"I don't think I've ever seen anyone as beautiful as you are," he said, extending his arm to receive her.

"Thank you, Amo." Smiling graciously, Hittitaes allowed him to lead her to their place in the cortège.

Sier and Rachel stood at the head of the assembly; Amo and Hittitaes stepped into position slightly behind them.

Tilac's father, Albar, Captain of the Protectorate, and his mother, Liana, greeted Serena and her mother, Daphne. "You look splendid, dear!" Liana kissed both Serena's cheeks, and Albar placed Serena's slim hand in Tilac's.

Caden, Keeper of the Dimensional Games, and his wife Olivia warmly embraced Melanie. "We're delighted Raze's companion for the Unveiling is so very charming!" Olivia smiled.

"You make a handsome escort, son," Melanie's father, Palek, patted Raze on the back. Raze dutifully accepted Melanie's hand in his own as they followed the remaining participants to assume their places.

The symbolic exchanges between the progenitors ended. The couples crossed the temple floor and stood before the entrance to the outer sanctuary.

Family and guests gathered in behind the couples and prepared for the opening of the sanctuary doors. Excited murmurs swept through the crowd.

"The gowns are marvelous!"

"How handsome and gallant the escorts are!"

Again the chiming of bells signaled the next stage of the ceremony. Voices hushed. Slowly and silently, the imposing doors swung open, revealing the white-gold walls of the outer sanctuary awash with light from the apex. Fluted columns flanked the doors along the chamber's exterior walls. They stood regally, the majestic drape of sparkling gossamer and wreaths of colorful blossoms gathered beneath ornate capitals. The aromatic fragrance of the flowers lightly scented the air.

A large platform had been erected on more fluted columns at the far end of the chamber. Their silvery shapes of the trees provided a magnificent backdrop to the stage. Steps carved from the purest white stone led from the floor of the chamber to the platform where Spatium's venerated leaders stood on ivory pedestals. At the center of the dais stood an ornate throne carved from a single, stunning emerald. Sapphire blue liquid cascaded down either side of the steps and splashed into fountained pools.

Heirs to Spatium's leadership moved in a stately procession to the far end of the chamber standing in front of the stage as the rest of the assembly filed in and took seats behind them.

"Esteemed citizens of Spatium," Caasi's voice reverberated throughout the chamber as he welcomed the participants, their families, and guests. "During this sacred portion of the ceremony, Spatium's heirs will be formally advanced to the level of Achiever. I have the honor of consecrating them to their responsibilities, as such, to contribute to the well-being of Spatium."

As their names were announced, each escort led his lady up

the stone stairs to kneel before the emerald throne. There they accepted accolades proffered upon them by the council and received commendations to their chosen professions.

Tears flowed in the audience as each of the heirs pledged on oath to give themselves wholly and faithfully to the mate that the FINISHER would, in his providence, bestow.

The Sons of Caasi were called, and together they escorted Rachel and Hittitaes to the platform to receive honor and blessing and to make their symbolic pledge.

Beaming, Spiritus gave thanks for his daughter Rachel, invoking favor and wisdom in the life awaiting her. "May you joyfully serve as wife, mother, and honored, productive citizen of Spatium."

Next, Caduceus' eyes brimmed with tears as he pronounced similar blessings upon Hittitaes. He offered praise for her beauty and invoked peace and prosperity upon her husband and her home.

"My dearest Hittitaes," Caduceus said, "may you always receive the desires of your heart!"

Caasi stepped forward to bless his sons. "I now have the honor of bestowing upon my two sons, the symbol of their heritage, and to thereby encourage them to pursue lives rich in service to the FINISHER." He held a platinum circle between his fingers and raised it above his head. The ring was widened and flattened at one end, where a single violet-purple stone rested, carved in the shape of a branching tree. He turned the ring in his fingers, sending shards of light, glinting off the many facets of the stone.

"My beloved Sier and Amo," Caasi said, "this ring marks you as treasured sons of the House of Caasi. May its symbolism spur you to great deeds of honor and service!"

The hall erupted with the sound of applause. When the ovation died down, Caasi went on.

"The circle of platinum represents unity, prosperity, and strength. Pursue them each with wisdom. The purple stone tree symbolizes the majestic sovereignty and steadfast love of the FINISHER," Caasi said, holding the ring aloft. "Strive always to be obedient to him. May the roots of the tree inspire you to pursue deep knowledge of him through the study of his book of Fabula and Syuzhet. Lead all of Spatium to follow him, and let his influence flow through you like sap through its branches."

Caasi paused and heaved a thoughtful sigh. "Ultimately, the tree is a tree of sacrifice—lay aside selfish ambition for the good of Spatium and the glory of the FINISHER, that he would reward you richly of his own accord. Finally, the power of the ring is to amplify the will of your heart; therefore, be mindful to keep its desires pure."

Caasi motioned for Amo to step forward. As he knelt, Caasi placed a hand on his son's head and began speaking.

"My dear son, Amo, it is my privilege to give you this ring, and to present you to all of Spatium, a treasured Son of the House of Caasi!"

Amo stood and held out a trembling right hand. Caasi slipped the ring on Amo's third finger, where it shone brightly with the symbol of his family line. He and Hittitaes moved to the right of the platform to stand with the other couples.

A hush fell over the audience as Caasi motioned for Sier to approach and kneel. The assembly held its collective breath in anticipation of his words.

"Sier, my son, my firstborn, I am honored to present you with this ring..." Caasi paused as Sier lifted his head and held forth his hand to receive the ring—his ring—that bore the mark of his father's house.

Caasi slipped the circlet onto the third finger of Sier's right hand

and continued, "...and to now present you to all of Spatium as ruling heir to the House of Caasi!"

The hall erupted in thunderous applause as Caasi raised Sier to his feet before the emerald throne.

Smiling, Caasi extended his hand toward Rachel, who was still kneeling and touched her bowed head. After a moment, the assembly quieted, unsure what to make of Caasi's gesture, or of Rachel, continuing to kneel under his hand.

Serena and Melanie moved closer to where Hittitaes stood beside Amo. Their eyes darted anxiously from her stoic face to the scene unfolding on the platform.

Caasi began speaking. "It is with unspeakable joy that I at this moment proclaim the Spatian daughter before me—"

Rachel trembled slightly at the pronouncement she knew was to come.

He continued, "...a woman of a keen mind, serene beauty and noble birth..."

Rachel thought of her mother, Aurora, who had been translated into the presence of the FINISHER, and wished she were here, or that she herself had been taken instead. Silent tears slipped down her cheeks. She listened as Caasi made the declaration and prepared to rise to her feet next to Sier.

"...Rachel Spiritus will join the House of Caasi as wife to Sier!" Caasi said.

Caasi lifted Rachel's chin with his hand, and she stood. Collective whispers and nods of approval rippled through the audience as Caasi went on.

"The ceremony of this Unveiling marks the beginning of their betrothal," he said. He made a show of turning Sier and Rachel to face the assembly. He placed Rachel's hand in Sier's and raised both in the air.

The chamber exploded in a burst of cheers and applause as everyone celebrated the double blessing.

"Can you believe it!" Melanie nudged Serena and whispered. "That should be Hittitaes there with Sier!"

Sier watched from the dais as Hittitaes whispered briefly to Amo, then quietly exited the chamber and headed toward the balconies surrounding the temple's outer court. He and Rachel continued to smile and accept congratulations as a host of Spatians wished them well.

True Unveiling

CHAPTER 23

Hittitaes stood in the shadows of the balcony overlooking the outer sanctuary. She allowed her tears to flow, unchecked. The ceremony ended and the chamber overflowed with Spatians celebrating the occasion and the betrothal of Sier to Rachel. Dancing, feasting, and merrymaking were the sole pursuits of every heart in the temple, except hers.

Turning her back on the celebration, she walked over to a large diaphanous pane in the outer wall of the pyramid. A breathtaking view of the landscape surrounding the temple lay before her.

She wasn't sure if it was cold hatred she felt for Rachel, or something far worse—a dispassionate apathy with which she could easily imagine Rachel simply gone, replaced by an image of herself in Sier's arms.

"Hittitaes!" Sier's voice interrupted her dark thoughts.

Instantly he was beside her, crossing the distance from the stairs to where she stood in a heartbeat.

Sier gathered Hittitaes in his arms and covered her face with kisses.

"I saw you leaving. I hoped I'd find you!" He cradled her tear-streaked face in his hands.

"What are you doing here?" Hittitaes shook her head and

looked up into Sier's eyes. "You should be celebrating with your fiancée."

"Hittitaes, there's something undeniable between us. I don't care what my father and Spiritus have arranged; I will follow my own heart," Sier said.

"Would you make me an adulteress?" she said, her voice rising. "I will not be your mistress, Sier!"

"I promise I will find a way for us to be together," he said.

"Are your words more powerful than your father's?" Hittitaes challenged. "Would you reject all that is yours as the firstborn son of Caasi? Would you defy his decree that Spiritus' daughter is to be your wife?"

Sier held Hittitaes away from himself, unwilling to let her go, yet unable to deny the truth of her questions. Her bare arms burned under his hands. The purple gem of his ring sparkled in the dim light.

He stared at the symbol of the House of Caasi for a long moment. Just as Hittitaes moved to free herself from his embrace, Sier lifted his right hand and removed the ring of his heritage from his finger.

∞

The sound of footsteps and the worried voices of Serena and Melanie advancing up the stairs to the balcony interrupted Sier and Hittitaes' passionate embrace.

"I have to go." Hittitaes indulged Sier in a last, lingering kiss before turning to hurry out of the shadows. She met her friends at the top of the stairs.

"There you are! We've been looking all over for you!" Serena rushed forward, taking Hittitaes' hand.

"You dear thing," Melanie crooned. "At least you look less upset, but your poor cheeks are flushed! Let's go down and get something to drink..."

Sier remained in the shadows of the balcony as the voices receded, blending in with the sounds of revelry floating up from the sanctuary. He sighed, looking out over the Spatian countryside.

"Sier!" Startled, Sier turned his attention from the window.

He faced the luminous white entity that had visited him at the Dimensional Games.

∞

"You look ...amazing!" Amo smiled his admiration for Rachel. He suddenly felt awkward in her presence. His heart raced, and his breath came in shallow gasps. Embarrassed, he looked away, surprised by the intensity of his attraction.

She returned his attention with a shrug. "Thanks, but shouldn't you be saving your compliments for your date?"

"Look, I don't want to get into another argument with you over her." Amo sighed. "I just want to apologize for acting like a fool... again."

Rachel managed a weak smile of her own. His apology marked a necessary change in their friendship. She resigned herself to the fact, but the realization made her sad.

Amo, seemed to read her mind. "So, it's official. You and my brother are to be married," he said.

Rachel nodded her head, her eyes downcast. There was nothing to say.

Amo tried to shake off the feeling that an unnamed presence hovered on the edge of his senses.

"Hey," Amo leaned in conspiratorially, "it looks like neither of our dates is around. Come on, there's no reason we shouldn't enjoy the party. I know you can dance."

He jerked his head slightly in the direction of the crowded platform. Several couples rocked and swayed to the music.

Rachel eyed him quizzically. She hesitated only briefly before taking Amo's hand, and with a mischievous gleam in her eye, replied, "Why not?" They raced up the stairs to join the others.

∞

"What are you doing here?" Sier demanded, warily approaching the white figure.

"You have not located the Meta symbols," came the toneless reply.

"What does that matter to you?" Sier shot back. "Do you have some vested interest in my success?"

The stranger's face twisted in a sardonic smile. "Perhaps," he drawled.

Sier leaned in close, his voice registering his frustration. "Then help me!" he insisted.

"Soon enough. But you must obtain the Meta symbols on your own."

∞

Hittitaes clutched Sier's ring, hidden in her palm and suspended from one of the long filigree strands that graced her neck. She had been watching Rachel pirouette under Amo's uplifted arm. Her anger smoldered like a carefully tended fire. She noticed that the ring in her hand seemed to heat up in concert with her emotion. She glanced toward the buffet; Serena and Melanie were still busy selecting delicacies from amid the sumptuous fare. She stole a peek at the ring hidden in the curve of her hand.

∞

"I'm tired of your games! If you won't help me, then stay out of my way!" Sier moved to shove the white-robed figure aside, but the stranger deftly maneuvered out of his way.

Sier's momentum sent him sprawling to the floor. He was vaguely aware of an electric hum reverberating throughout the room. The sound was like ominous laughter.

Enraged, Sier scrambled to his feet and lunged toward the stranger in white. Again, the being sidestepped the charge, and Sier went crashing toward the window like a lumbering beast.

Rolling onto his back, Sier hurled a white-hot sphere of energy toward the creature, who vanished before his eyes.

The heated plasma ball whizzed through the air and beyond the arch. Beads of cold sweat broke out on Sier's brow. The flaming orb was headed for one of the massive decorated columns towering over the celebrants below.

∞

Hittitaes saw the fireball before she heard it. It made an awful hissing sound as it streaked toward a pillar near the crowded stage turned dance floor.

117

∞

The g lowing sphere s lammed w ith e xplosive f orce i nto t he massive column above where Amo and Rachel danced, then careened into the wall. The crowd scattered in all directions, separating him from Rachel in the panic.

Amo looked up to see what was left of the top third of the pillar pitch forward and begin its sickening descent toward the floor. He realized with horror that the massive chunk of debris was headed for the very spot where Rachel stood. Without thinking, he shoved his hands out toward her with all of his strength.

Unnoticed in the chaos, a silvery beam of energy flashed across the room. It slammed into Rachel, hurling her backward and out of the path of the crumbling stone. She landed, pinned against the bottom of the pillar.

"No!" Amo yelled. He was sure that in trying to save Rachel, he had instead doomed her to be crushed beneath the rubble.

He willed the air around her to solidify, praying he'd created a shield strong enough to protect her.

He couldn't escape the feeling that something moved among the throng, just beyond his ability to perceive it, watching the disaster unfold. A deadly shower began to rain down on the stage.

∞

Sier's stomach lurched and clenched into an impossibly tight knot as he stared helplessly at the fireball streaking toward the massive column.

The blinding light and deafening sound of the explosion spurred him to action. Sier raced from the shadows and leaned out over the balustrade. Spreading his hands, he energized the air above the chamber into an impenetrable shield.

Its shaft splintered, the ornate capital of the massive column continued to fall, shattering on impact with the invisible plane of energy. Helpless, the terrified Spatians continued to kneel, arms shielding their heads as they braced for the impending blows, unaware that the rain of debris had been halted.

After a long moment, people stopped running, lowered their arms, and began to look up from where they cowered. Shouts of joy erupted as the miracle of their salvation dawned on them. Someone pointed beyond the life-saving canopy to a lone figure stretched out over the balcony, a shield of pure energy emanating from his outstretched hands.

The soft sound of voices lifted in thanks steadily rose, until the people's praise swelled to a crescendo that reached Sier's ears above the energy flowing from his fingertips.

Caasi's Farewell

CHAPTER 24

Sier stepped inside his father's study and closed the door behind him. Caasi looked up from his desk and motioned for Sier to take a seat.

Riva heard the door to Caasi's study close. She walked over from the kitchen and paused outside to listen. She frowned, thinking it odd that Caasi had not mentioned having a visitor. She was unaware that Sier had returned.

"You wanted to see me, father?" Sier asked.

"Yes, my son." Caasi took a deep breath and delivered his next words soberly and without preamble. "My purpose on Spatium is near completion."

Sier's gasp was loud in the quiet of the room.

Caasi went on, ignoring his reaction. "My Translation is near. Soon, I am to depart for the presence of the FINISHER."

Sier felt his heart racing, and a light sweat slicked his palms. His stomach tensed in anticipation of his father's words.

"I have made it clear what I believe. As my firstborn son, you are ordained by the FINISHER to be the Time-Ruler," Caasi said. He paused, drilling Sier with his gaze. His next words would make the decision irrevocable.

"Your actions at the Unveiling have affirmed my intentions,

Caasi said. "I will present you the cup of Zhù Fú. My highest blessing is to be yours."

"I assure you I am worthy!" Sier lept to his feet before Caasi. "This is my purpose. My authority will know no bounds!" He made no effort to suppress his delight. "I will rule all of the FINISHER's creation!"

Caasi sat, momentarily stunned by Sier's hubris. "My son, beware of pride and refrain from arrogance—"

"Father, I forget myself," Sier Of course, I am saddened by your imminent departure," Sier said.

His son's words rang hollowly in Caasi's ears. Sier's feigned remorse stung less than the thinly veiled conceit that was certain to be his downfall. His jaw set, Caasi warily regarded Sier over the tips of his tented fingers. "I will make the announcement to the Royal Council at the Hall of Letters," he said.

"Thank you, Father." Standing, Sier nodded and left the room.

Riva quickly stepped into the recesses of the hallway as Sier exited Caasi's study. Her mind reeling, she silently prayed to the FINISHER. She asked his forgiveness for what was in her heart to do.

∞

Sier retrieved the temple articles he'd stolen from where he'd hidden them in his room. After a quick check of the upstairs hall, he jauntily strolled to Amo's room and tossed the bundle inside, where it landed beneath the bed.

∞

"I stand before you both elated with joy and weighed down by a heavy heart."

Caasi stood to address the members of the Royal Council of Spatium from his place at the emerald table.

"I have enjoyed a full and prosperous life," he said.

"As a Seeker, the desire to know the will of the FINISHER consumed me. The only thing that tore me away from my studies," he said with an owlish wink, "was the gift of my beautiful wife, Riva. She has shared my passion for the things of the FINISHER and made our house a beautiful home. Together we have raised two sons to the level of Seeker and Achiever. I invoke blessings upon them as they embark on the most significant journeys in life—marrying, maturing, raising their own families, learning, and applying wisdom as many of us have done. I pray they will prosper as Achievers and serve Spatium well when they become its Pillars. I have served and enjoyed the requisite struggles and triumphs of both. Now, I stand before you at the Point of Zenith."

He sighed, reverently lifting his hands. "My departure from you is imminent. Soon I will bow humbly in the very presence of the FINISHER." His voice shook with emotion even as he raised his eyes toward the crystal apex above the Hall of Letters. He seemed to gaze far beyond the enclosure of the pyramid; his sight focussed with awe on a vision the others could not see. "I will soon be translated." He tore his eyes from whatever scene had held him captive and returned his attention to the council.

Spiritus, Caduceus, Sophia, and the others listened with rapt attention. The full membership was present, including Albar, Captain of the Protectorate, Instructor Em Sartor, Caden and

Daphne, Keepers of the Dimensional Games, and the Recorders, Palek, and Rex.

"Give ear! These are my last official acts as leader of the Royal Council of Spatium," Caasi continued. Gone was the reverent quaver from his speech, replaced by the resonant and authoritative voice of Spatium's most powerful ruler.

"As has been said, the houses of Caasi and Spiritus will be united through the covenant marriage of my firstborn son Sier, to Rachel, the noble and virtuous daughter of Spiritus," Caasi said.

Tomos and Malaika led the applause as the sound of their generous ovation filled the chamber. Caduceus responded coolly, acknowledging the announcement with perfunctory applause.

"It is my intent that the merging of our bloodlines and authority will ensure unwavering loyalty to the FINISHER." The room quieted as Caasi continued, "I hereby appoint my son Sier heir to my seat on the Royal Council. May he ultimately attain all of its rights, responsibilities, and privileges, and inspire you to elect him your leader. May he always champion your adherence to the prophecies as revealed in the book of Fabula and Syuzhet."

Palek and Rex rose to address the council.

"Honorable Caasi, your official last acts as leader of the Royal Council of Spatium," they said in unison—

"have been heard," said Palek.

"and recorded," said Rex.

"This is a glorious occasion for the House of Caasi!" Caasi spread his arms wide. "You all are invited to join our family as I seal my decree with the presentation of the cup of Zhù fú to my son Sier."

The din of applause masked the electrifying hum of Caduceus' inner calculations. Caasi had indeed bequeathed his seat on the Council to Sier, but the naming of his bride was another matter.

∞

"I'm sorry about what happened to Rachel." Caasi embraced Spiritus warmly. "We are all praying for her recovery."

"I appreciate your prayers, dear friend." They stood apart from the others to talk. Their conversation was occasionally interrupted as Caasi accepted well-wishes from exiting council members.

"Please forgive what I feel compelled to say," Spiritus began. "I certainly had hoped not to darken this celebration of your leadership—"

"Come, dear friend," Caasi said, waving a dismissive hand. "We are beyond such trifles. Speak your mind."

"You're aware I have been teaching Sier to master his skills..." Spiritus' voice trailed off. "I have also been working with Amo."

"Whatever for?" Caasi asked.

"I apologize for not sharing this with you," Spiritus said. "Amo has extraordinary abilities. I thought I could be of help to him in learning to control them."

"I see." Caasi nodded, regarding Spiritus steadily.

"I also thought that in training Amo, I might help him find a place of service to Sier, The Time-Ruler," Spiritus said.

Caasi leveled a questioning gaze at his friend. He wondered if Spiritus would pit one of his sons against the other, and to what end?

"Unfortunately," Spiritus continued, "I underestimated Amo's desire to surpass his brother, and perhaps usurp him to become Time-Ruler himself."

Caasi responded with raised eyebrows.

"I believe Amo attempted to deceive me by manipulating the training simulator," Spiritus said. "The impossible measurements it recorded, if true, would mean Amo's abilities exceed that of Sier's by untold orders of magnitude. He would challenge Sier's reign as Time-Ruler."

"You are indeed wise, my friend," sighed Caasi. He raised a hand to stroke his beard. "Perhaps I have devoted my attention to Sier at the expense of Amo's integrity."

"My heart breaks for you as a father, Caasi." Spiritus heaved a sigh of his own. "I value our friendship, but in light of his deception and to protect the treaty, I must insist that Amo stay away from Rachel."

"To preserve the union of our houses," Caasi responded, "and by the will of the FINISHER, I assure you, Amo will heed your wishes."

Journey to Earth

CHAPTER 25

"Thank you for inviting me to join you in the temple, father," Amo said as he and Caasi approached the arch of the Protectors.

"Your passion for the things of the FINISHER is admirable, my son," Caasi said. He greeted the temple guards with a nod. He and Amo entered the court of the Hall of Letters.

Amo marveled at the gems embedded in the walls of the temple.

"Do the Protectors guard the wealth of the temple, father? Does Spatium so value its treasures?" he asked.

"The FINISHER needs no guard, my son. He is omnipotent." Caasi smiled indulgently at Amo. A hint of sadness pulled the corners of his mouth downward. "The Protectors are his angels, much like Malaika. They stand ready to deliver the message of his will. They are a symbol of his protection over us."

Father and son walked on in silence. They passed through the massive doors of the outer sanctuary. Amo absently commented on the splendor of the place. The carnage of the Unveiling had been cleared and the beauty of the outer chamber restored. He wondered if that was what had prompted Caasi's invitation.

"It is said that all the treasure of the FINISHER's creation rests here to remind us that everything belongs to him. Our wealth, our power, we ourselves are at his disposal," Caasi said, resuming the conversation. "We exist to do his good pleasure."

"Are we merely pawns to be manipulated, regardless of our will?" Amo asked.

"Dear Amo," Caasi said patiently, "even our will belongs to him. We are free in him to do and to be more than we ever could alone."

Amo looked doubtful as he and Caasi continued past the columns and doors toward the silvery copse under the arch. "The FINISHER seems so distant." Amo said.

"The Hall of Letters is the FINISHER's dwelling place here in Spatium," Caasi explained. "Although he is never far, we are a little closer to him here—"

"It doesn't matter where I am," Amo interrupted. "His prophecies have no meaning for me!"

"The FINISHER has his purposes to accomplish through our lives," Caasi said.

"What should that mean to me, father?" Amo's voice rose in frustration. "So, what difference does it make what I do?"

"Whatever you do, you are to maintain your integrity and the honor of the name of Caasi—" Caasi began.

"I haven't done anything to tarnish your name!" Amo said, his face flushed with anger.

"Spiritus says otherwise," Caasi countered. "He claims you manipulated the training simulator to deceive him!"

Amo's mouth hung open in disbelief. He fumbled for words, and Caasi concluded that he had indeed caught Amo in his deceit.

"Why, Amo?" Caasi asked. "Were you hoping to convince Spiritus that you have greater power than Sier? Did you think that somehow he would take your side and recommend you to be Time-Ruler over your brother?"

Speechless, Amo compressed his lips in a tight, angry line.

"Spiritus has requested that you distance yourself from Rachel," Caasi said. "I am ordering you to obey his wishes."

They stood before the book of Fabula and Syuzhet, Caasi's tirade silenced by the sudden activity of the book. The sacred tome came alive in a furious rush of fluttering pages.

Caasi caught his son in his arms as Amo collapsed in a dead faint.

∞

The floor of the temple rushed up to meet him, but instead sped past, transformed into inky blackness dotted with celestial bodies orbiting spheres of burning gas. Amo hurtled across the vast, cold emptiness of the space toward a terrestrial ball unlike any of the others whizzing by.

Suddenly, he was immersed in an unfamiliar atmosphere. Beneath him, elongated metallic birds with rows of eyes on either side of their bodies soared in a blue sky. Light radiating from an enormous superheated ball of plasma illuminated the planet below.

Rushing over a sea of blue teeming with creatures both large and small, Amo found himself enjoying the study of them even as he was being driven along on the wind. As soon as he'd begun to think of their names, they were gone, replaced by a stretch of what he assumed was land.

Shifting and dry, rolling and lush, peaked and cratered, the land spread out beneath him. Groups of geometric structures dotted its surface. Winding roads and looming edifices huddled together along with ribbons of blue that cut the land.

Hordes of carbon-based life forms milled about. Amo could see them now. They held bars of flickering light in front of their faces or against their ears when they spoke.

And then, in an instant, he felt it—an overwhelming sense of pure being. He gasped for breath, smothered by the intensity of billions of souls bearing down upon him. Bodies scrambled about at a dizzying pace, barely interacting with one another, though they crowded the patches of land they inhabited.

Suddenly the beings appeared to notice Amo. Billions of faces turned toward him, as he hovered, suspended above them. Countless pairs of eyes stared intently, boring into him. The clamor of their voices rose in unison, some shouting, some shrieking, all demanding an answer to the same question.

"Who will save us?"

Treachery Blooms

CHAPTER 26

Sier waited anxiously for Hittitaes to arrive at their secret trysting place. He knew that their meetings would disgrace both of their families if they were discovered, and yet he was powerless to resist his desire to be with her.

Yet he was bound by his father's covenant to Rachel. She hadn't awakened from her injuries at the Unveiling, and the thought that she might not survive gave him mixed feelings of sadness and hope.

Hittitaes suddenly appeared, breathless in her haste to reach him. All thoughts of Rachel fled as he took Hittitaes into his arms.

∞

Riva entered the garden. Amo sat on a bench, his head buried in his hands. She had been desperate to speak with him since she'd overheard the conversation between Caasi and Sier. With neither her husband nor Sier at home, she seized the opportunity.

"Amo, I must speak with you," she called to him.

"Yes, Mother?" Amo lifted his head. His eyes settled on his mother where she stood near a white flowering trellis.

"May I join you?" she asked.

"Of course," Amo said. "Please, come, sit down."

Amo stood and ushered his mother across the garden to the bench where he'd been sitting.

"I must be blunt, and you must trust me, even if you don't understand," she began. "Your father will soon be translated to the FINISHER."

Amo sharply drew in a breath. Mixed emotions swept over him. To stand in the presence of the FINISHER was the ultimate goal of every Spatian's existence, but the thought of the absence of his father here, in this place, left him numb. Tears welled up in his eyes, and he sat, silent until they spilled down his cheeks.

"He plans to give the cup of Zhù fú to Sier," Riva announced.

"Mother," Amo sighed, wiping away his tears in exasperation, "Sier is to be Time-Ruler. I can't change that. What does the cup matter?"

"Dearest Amo, the cup of Zhù fú is far more important than you know. Its blessing is irrevocable." She wrung her hands and shifted on the seat. "Sier seeks power, not truth. He cares neither for the will of the FINISHER nor for the meaning of the prophecies." Her eyes darted toward the house to be certain they would not be surprised by Caasi or Sier returning home. "You, Amo, are a seeker of truth. The FINISHER's will is the guidepost of your life."

She raised a hand to halt the objection forming on Amo's lips. "And yet this is not only about you," she continued, "but about Spatium and the FINISHER's new creation. I cannot explain it, but I fear that for Sier to receive the blessing is to doom us all."

"Mother, what would you suggest I do?" Amo asked. "Father will not simply have a change of heart and give the cup of his blessing to me." Impatience crept around the edges of his voice. "He is convinced that I tried to deceive Spiritus—"

"No, he won't give it to you, Amo," she interrupted. Her voice was eerily tranquil, her demeanor the embodiment of patience. Riva exhaled a long sigh. Her shoulders relaxed as though accepting the weight of an unseen burden.

"But he will give the cup to Sier," she said.

Amo's confused look did not deter her. Riva took his hands and held them gently in her lap. He leaned forward, listening wide-eyed even as her words filled him with dread.

∞

"What are those?" Caasi asked. Riva balanced several books in one hand and some clothing items in the other. She and Caasi had been tidying up the family room.

"They appear to be books." She smiled, flipping open a few covers. "They're Amo's," she said. "Would you mind putting them back in his room for me?"

"Sure." Caasi returned her smile. "Where is Amo, anyway?" He headed upstairs to his son's room.

"I sent him on some errands," Riva called after him.

Caasi dropped one of the books as he placed them on a bookcase. Bending to retrieve it, he looked twice before reaching under the bed, his face contorting in anger. He stood up, clutching a satchel embellished with the insignia of the Hall of Letters.

"Riva!" he bellowed. "Riva! You need to see this!"

Breathless, Riva rushed into Amo's room to find Caasi livid. The satchel and its contents lay atop Amo's bed.

"These were stolen from the Hall of Letters!" Caasi shouted, pointing to the sacred objects.

"It must be a mistake." Riva's voice was a shocked whisper.

"What kind of mistake could it be? It's obvious—"

"But Caasi, why would he do such a thing?" Riva asked. She posed the question more to herself than to her husband. "I don't know!" she said.

"Maybe his obsession with the temple isn't about the prophecy, after all." Caasi's unspoken accusation hung in the air between them.

"Our son is not a thief!" Riva spoke first.

"Riva," Caasi said, placing his hands on his wife's shoulders. "I need to say something." He sighed heavily, pained by her anxious frown. "Spiritus saw something in Amo... a tremendous potential. He thought he could encourage Amo by mentoring him, by helping him develop his unique abilities." Caasi hesitated and took a deep breath before going on. "Amo attempted to deceive Spiritus into believing that he is powerful enough to challenge Sier's right to be Time-Ruler."

Riva was silent. She shook her head in disbelief.

"Spiritus will no longer help Amo," Caasi said. "He's also forbidden him to see Rachel."

Riva's face was downcast. "I don't believe it!"

"I didn't want to believe it either, Riva. But with this—" he spread his hands, indicating the items on Amo's bed. "I'm not sure what to believe."

"He's our son, Caasi!" Riva said. "Shouldn't we be giving him the benefit of the doubt?"

"His obsession with the prophecy may be clouding his judgment. Why else would he try to trick Spiritus into thinking there could be some doubt about Sier's birthright?" Caasi's stern look silenced Riva's protest.

"When I took him to the Hall of Letters, he fainted dead away from guilt before the book of Fabula and Syuzhet!"

Riva remained silent.

"Riva! These things were stolen from the temple," Caasi said. "There is no doubt about that! Surely there is a limit to your ability to overlook Amo's deception?"

Caasi gathered the items from Amo's bed and left the room.

Riva's icy gaze melted. Soon, the sound of her quiet weeping filled the silence.

∞

"What is the meaning of this?" Caasi sat in his study and glared at Amo over the temple articles spread neatly across his desk.

"Aren't they from the Hall of Letters?" Amo asked, his eyes wide.

"Don't pretend you've never seen them!" Caasi pounded the arm of his chair with a fist.

Startled, Amo spread his hands. "Father, I swear to you, I—"

"Enough! I will not suffer you to lie to my face!" Caasi's next words were tinged with grief. "Amo, my son, could you not rejoice over your brother's blessing with us? There will be but one Time-Ruler. Would you waste your life fighting for that which belongs to your brother? Or will you make your own calling and election sure?"

Amo's face darkened. He struggled to keep his emotions under control. His father had pronounced judgment on him. Amo could tell by the unflinching set of Caasi's jaw that he had made up his mind. Amo's guilt was settled.

Caasi straightened in his chair. "You will return these things to the Hall of Letters, at once."

At that moment, Amo decided he would go through with his mother's plan. And now, her idea gave him one of his own.

He had not stolen the items from the Hall of Letters, but before all of Spatium, he would take away the honor both Caasi and Sier prized most.

The Mask
CHAPTER 27

"A challenge has been issued. You have been called upon to defend your title as Champion of the Dimensional Games." The large gymnasium of the Axle was empty except for Sier and the blazing white figure.

"By whom?" Sier scoffed. "I will take on any challenger!"

"Your father's greatest nemesis has been released from Containment," the white figure spoke again. "He is determined to avenge his loss and imprisonment."

Sier recalled that in his father's final appearance in the Dimensional Games, controversy erupted over cheating by one of his challengers. The result was that the combatant had been sentenced to Containment until he had completed several punitive tasks.

"Your confidence is admirable, Sier," the stranger said, interrupting his thoughts. "However, be aware that for you to be defeated in this challenge would cause speculation about the certainty of your right to reign as Time-Ruler."

"That's ridiculous!" Sier glared. "No one would dare challenge me! I am firstborn to the House of Caasi. To be enthroned as Time-Ruler is my birthright!" Now shouting, his voice echoed throughout the gymnasium.

"The prophecy promises that "a son of Caasi" will embody the enigma of time and reign sovereignly over the FINISHER's new creation." The visitor paused before adding, gravely, "It is your father's decision that the prophecy refers to you."

Sier's temples throbbed with rage. He was nearly blinded by the urge to hurl all of the energy at his disposal toward the glowing entity. He held back, the exploding column at the Unveiling an all too fresh reminder of the result of giving in to such an impulse.

"What exactly are you implying?" Sier demanded through gritted teeth.

"The implication is this," ignoring Sier's outburst, the stranger leaned forward menacingly, "You hesitate to secure the Meta symbols at your own peril! A defeat in this challenge could lead to open questioning of your right to rule! Your conqueror would seize the opportunity to amass a following of his own and challenge the very right to power you wield so carelessly!"

The sound of Sier's tortured, angry breathing filled the room.

"Another contender has also arisen," the stranger continued, "but his identity is unknown."

∞

Sier and the challengers to his standing as champion stood on the dais and waited for the opening ceremony of this round of Spatium's Dimensional Games to begin. As champion, Sier was obligated to take on all challengers to his title. He turned to look directly at the other two combatants, openly sizing them up. Absently, he flexed his biceps, sending an intimidating ripple through the muscle.

Silikon was stockily built, his sightless eyes level with Sier's chin. If opened, anyone looking into them would be instantly encased in stone—alive, but trapped in a prison of his own hardened skin. Silikon's wife often boasted that many of her husband's opponents now adorned the halls of their palatial home. Alternating sounds of tortured screams and pitiful whimpering filled its corridors with a macabre symphony of despair.

Silikon nearly defeated Caasi in a hotly contested round, but was disqualified and then incarcerated for cheating. Vehemently denying any wrongdoing, Silikon vowed to exact revenge on Caasi. Defeating Sier would be a satisfying step in that direction, he thought.

Duty-bound to defend his father's honor, Sier was bent on conquering Silikon. He also relished the opportunity to prove himself a better warrior than Caasi by facing and soundly defeating his father's nemesis.

Mask was a newcomer who hid his identity behind a shiny, black visor. He had shown himself a capable opponent in the preliminary exercises. No matter, Sier thought. Many of the spectators believed Mask was a foil, inserted to prevent the dignity of the tournament from being reduced to a grudge match. Seeing his reflection in the polished blackness, Sier narrowed his eyes and glared, snorting defiantly before returning his attention to the crowd. The contest was about to begin.

Excitement reverberated throughout the arena. Scattered chants of "Sier!" broke out among the spectators as the combatants waited to take their places on the field.

∞

Caasi and Riva were seated in a lavish pavilion specially erected for members of the Royal Council and other dignitaries. The private boxes they usually occupied were gifted at random to hundreds of lucky Spatian citizens for this event.

"Daphne will keep a close eye on Silikon," Caasi commented. Daphne was already on the arena floor. Caden, her counterpart as Keeper of the Dimensional Games occupied the official observation booth at the far side of the pavilion.

Caasi had noticed Riva's intense scrutiny of every aspect of his former adversary's behavior since they'd arrived. The half-moons of her nails imprinted her palms where she'd dug them into the flesh.

Caduceus entered the pavilion and stopped to address Caasi and Riva on his way to his seat. "May your son fight well," he said, effecting a slight bow.

"Thank you," Caasi replied. "Sier is a skilled fighter."

"True," Caduceus agreed, "though he may have his hands full with Silikon."

"I believe this challenge is a good thing," Caasi said. "A victory for Sier will be very satisfying."

"Silikon is a fine warrior. He will no doubt prove the mettle of the prophesied Time-Ruler." Caduceus dropped the barb then moved quickly to join Hittitaes, a few rows behind them.

"Caduceus' presence unnerves me," Riva whispered. "Surely he has accepted his role on the Royal Council, as well as his defeat?"

Caduceus had failed in his attempt to usurp leadership of the Royal Council of Spatium from Caasi. He had lobbied council members and forced a vote to overthrow Caasi and install himself as head. In open debate, Caasi convinced the needed majority of the wisdom of faithfulness to the FINISHER and continued adherence to the prophecies of the book of Fabula and Syuzhet. He acknowledged that interpreting the book had grown increasingly difficult, but his argument hinged on the necessity of faith. In the end, the Council had rejected Caduceus' bid to overthrow him. Caasi was relieved to have successfully put down Caduceus' plan. Spatium would continue to rely on the prophetic dictates of the FINISHER.

Nonetheless, Caasi was well aware that the outcome had only served to inflame Caduceus' resentment.

Subsequently, Caasi and Spiritus had joined forces to silence Caduceus' frequent challenges to what he called Spatium's "blind loyalty to impotent prophecy." The hope was that the union of their houses would strengthen the council's resolve to withstand another attack by Caduceus on the fundamental principles governing Spatian life.

"Not to worry," Caasi said, patting his wife's hand. "Once Sier and Rachel are wed, Caduceus will realize that his schemes are futile. Spatium will continue as it always has, allied to the FINISHER and guided by his prophecies."

Riva smiled, but her husband's words did little to quiet the sense of foreboding that gnawed at her spirit. "Nevertheless," she murmured, "how dare he laud that scoundrel Silikon as a fine warrior!"

"Where is Amo?" Caasi ignored her comment craning his neck to scan the crowd. "He should be here. He'll miss the start of the Games!"

∞

Gameskeeper Caden stood to address the spectators and Spatium's elite from the front of the pavilion. The sound of his voice filled the arena, pleasantly amplified by its natural acoustics. "The tournament will unfold in three rounds," he began. "During the Challenger's

Round, contenders Silikon and Mask will fight each other in a demonstration of their tactical and metaphysical skill."

Caden paused, bowing slightly toward the challengers. "At the end of the Challenger's Round," he continued, "reigning champion, Sier Caasi will choose the order in which he will battle each of the challengers individually." Caden bowed long and deep, respectfully acknowledging Sier.

Sier eyed Silikon and the newcomer, Mask. He would carefully observe the Challenger's Round, noting each one's strengths and weaknesses. He could then wisely choose which of them to fight first in the Principal Round. If he lost to the first opponent, his rivals would then fight each other to determine his successor in the Champion's Round.

"Combatants, take your places!" Gameskeeper Caden signaled the start of the contest.

The battlefield was in the shape of an isosceles triangle. Sier took his place at its vertex, while each of the challengers moved to one of the angles formed along its base. Caasi, Riva, and Spatium's elite watched from the pavilion. Onlookers filled tiers of seats that ringed the floor and ascended to etch a circle on the cloudy sky. The arena brimmed with Spatians threatening to spill over its top.

Caden announced. "Let the Challenger's Round of these Dimensional Games begin!"

∞

Silikon and Mask advanced toward the center of the triangle, circling and eyeing each other for any sign of vulnerability. A charged plasma forcefield contained the combatants and protected onlookers from errant projectiles. Sier watched intently, keen to detect any clue as to which challenger to take on first.

Mask launched the opening attack, sending a sphere of energy hurtling through the air toward Silikon. Unfazed, Silikon reared back and allowed the fireball to pass through a hole that materialized in the center of his barrel-shaped chest.

In response, the sound of a howling wind whistled through the containment area, whipping around Silikon and dissolving his face, thick neck and muscular body into a whirling vortex of sand.

Steadily, the tornado shape advanced toward Mask until it enveloped him in a storm of razor-sharp bits that ripped at his skin like a thousand shards of glass.

Mask condensed the molecules of the air around him, protecting himself with an impenetrable shield that deflected the hailstorm surging around him. Silikon continued to rage against the barrier to no avail until finally he reconstituted himself and stood in front of Mask.

In an instant, Mask discharged the shield and launched himself at the surprised Silikon, slamming a fist into his midsection. Mask's clenched hand sunk wrist-deep into the miry clay of Silikon's abdomen. Caught off guard, but recovering quickly, Silikon began to solidify his form around Mask's fist, now stuck fast in the tightening web of his gut. Silikon pummeled Mask about the head and neck.

His visor absorbed most of the force from Silikon's blows, but Mask was sure he wouldn't be able to endure the punishment for long. The biting sand and swirling glass of Silikon's attack had given him an idea. He pretended to struggle to free himself long enough for Silikon to lock on to the bulk of his fist fully. He then focused all of his attention on creating a superheated fireball in the palm of his hand. Slowly but surely, the substance of Silikon's belly began to glow like molten glass.

The sound of a gong signaled the end of the round. Now, Sier would choose his first opponent.

∞

The Challenger's Round had revealed a vulnerability, but not in the way Sier had hoped. He now had to choose which opponent to battle first. Only one of them had shown a weakness he felt he could exploit.

Caden signaled for Sier to make his selection, and Sier marched forward to the center of the triangle. He announced the battle sequence. "I will crush Silikon first, and then do likewise to the veiled coward."

Mask and Silikon half-bowed toward Sier, then Mask retreated to his corner of the triangle to await the final battle. His stomach knotted involuntarily as Sier grunted, dismissing him.

"You've underestimated me, son of Caasi," Silikon snarled, grinding the stumps of teeth set in his powerful jaw. Offended at being chosen to do battle first, he repeatedly slammed a fist into his palm. Silikon figured that Sier thought him easier to defeat than the faceless newcomer, and so chose to engage him first. "I am not surprised that the son of a coward is a fool!" he shouted.

Silikon recalled his battle against Caasi in the Dimensional Games. Caasi detected the tell-tale aroma of a performance-enhancing stimulant and reported him to the lower game official, Daphne. Silikon openly called Caasi a coward for reporting him rather than continuing the fight like a true warrior. Caden, Keeper of the Dimensional Games, had launched an investigation and ultimately found Silikon guilty. He recommended to the Royal Council of Spatium that Silikon be incarcerated until he'd served the maximum sentence for the offense.

The memory scorched Silikon's already inflamed mind. Hungry to make Sier pay for Caasi's cowardice, the insult of being chosen to fight first was like a kick in the teeth.

"Let the Principal Round begin!" declared Caden.

Faster than it would seem possible for his squat body to move, Silikon catapulted toward Sier, startling him and knocking him to the ground.

Sier's head struck the arena floor with a sickening thud. Dazed, he feebly raised his arms to ward off Silikon's blows.

Capitalizing on Sier's confusion, Silikon moved his face to within inches of Sier's and lifted the lids of his hooded eyes. With all of his strength, Silikon landed a blow to Sier's midsection that audibly knocked the wind out of him.

Sier's eyes flew open. Disoriented, he stared into the blinding light of Silikon's luminous orbs and was instantly encased in stone.

Caasi and the other council members were on their feet in the pavilion. Stunned, Caduceus tried to quiet the screams of Hittitaes even as he wondered how the loss of Sier would impact his plans to take control of the Royal Council.

The silence of the crowd was shattered by a bloodcurdling howl of triumph that shook the arena to its foundations. Silikon raised his fists in victory.

Riva fainted.

Caden's efforts to restore order were just short of futile. Drunk with the win, Silikon swaggered across the arena floor, the stumps of his teeth exposed in a feral grin. Mask nearly wretched at the sight of Sier's body lying entombed on the arena floor. Silikon paraded around it in a shuffling, macabre combination of worship and contempt. Silikon turned toward the pavilion and gloated over his conquest. Leering before the horror-stricken face of Caasi, he planted a foot on Sier's chest.

Suddenly, the stone cocoon exploded from within, rocking the arena and catapulting Silikon into the air. Sier stood above him, unharmed; white bits of material speckled his skin and hair. Silikon's eyes were wide, his prideful glare replaced by one of terror. His mouth worked in fits, flecks of spittle spraying the air.

Pandemonium broke out in the stands. The spectators cheered wildly, whistling and chanting Sier's name.

Silikon landed on his back at Sier's feet. Reaching down, Sier grabbed Silikon's throat and lifted him until his feet kicked spasmodically above the ground. Silikon grasped frantically at Sier's fingers, tightly clasped about his neck.

Sier jerked Silikon's face to within inches of his own. He looked deeply into his wild eyes, shielding himself from their effect. He sent a blast of white-hot energy surging through his fingers and into Silikon's body, ending its spasms and turning Silikon into a crystal blue effigy of himself.

Lifting his trophy over his head with both hands, Sier slowly pivoted at the triangle's center. His display met with riotous applause and shouts mingled with the thunder of untold numbers of feet pounding the arena floor. Facing the pavilion, Sier stopped, searching for Caasi. Their eyes locked, and Sier could read the fathomless depths of pride in his father's eyes. With an earsplitting roar, he hurled the cerulean figure of Silikon to the ground, shattering it into a million pieces.

The stadium erupted in thunderous applause. Chants of "Sier! Sier!" swelled to an earsplitting crescendo.

Sier cocked his head and turned to face his final opponent. Mask readied himself for the battle.

∞

Caden once again stepped forward to announce the match.

"Ladies and Gentlemen of Spatium," he said, "prepare to witness the Champion's Round! The reigning champion of these Dimensional Games, Sier Caasi, will defend his title against the challenger, Mask. Let the Champion's Round begin!"

Sier immediately unleashed a plasma ball and sent it rocketing toward Mask. Ducking, Mask raised a shield and hurled a flaming sphere of his own. Sier adroitly avoided the white-hot projectile and framed the image of the quickly advancing Mask in the circle of his cupped palms. A transparent blue sphere materialized between his palms before vanishing and reappearing to surround Mask, halting his forward stride. A smug smile forming at the corners of his lips, Sier attempted to manipulate Mask's essence, much as he had Tilac in the Axle and then Rachel in the forest. His mouth fell open in surprise when Mask, after only the slightest hesitation, stepped outside Sier's trap, unfazed and unchanged.

Mask warily circled. He kept his sights on Sier. He feinted and parried, firing laser-like blasts and probing for any sign of vulnerability. There were none.

Sensing his opponent's lack of a kill strategy, Sier charged, overwhelming Mask with a barrage of missiles that pinned him to the ground under cover of his plasma shield.

Sier's energy was too strong, and Mask felt his defense weakening. Soon the shield would be breached, and the battle would be over. Mask began to regret his decision to challenge Sier.

The rain of missiles ended, but there was no relief. Sier stood, towering over him. He watched as Sier peered at him, crouched beneath a shield of pulsating energy. To his horror, Sier simply reached beyond the barrier and grabbed him by the neck. Sier choked him until he could hardly breath.

"And now, I will reveal your face!" Sier shouted. "Your defeat and your identity will live in infamy throughout Spatium!"

Fully intending to shatter any illusions Mask may have had of slinking off in anonymous defeat, Sier ripped the visor away. He gasped, suddenly face to face with his brother. Sier faltered, loosening his grip.

Amo threw Sier off, sending him staggering backward to land in a heap a few yards away. He rose shakily to his feet, staring first at his brother and then at Caasi and Riva, who watched in astonishment from beneath the pavilion.

Enraged, Sier rushed Amo. The two brothers collided with audible force. They fought, pummeling each other in a flailing mass of fists and elbows until they tumbled, wrestling, to the ground.

The crowd looked on in stunned silence as the sons of Caasi landed blow after blow upon each other's heads, faces, and bodies in a frenzy of unstopped emotion. Tears streaked their faces, their cries of anger and pain carried to the rim of the still amphitheater.

Sier finally pinned Amo beneath him. He raised a fist, poised to bring it crashing into his brother's face. The crowd stood, silent in anticipation.

"Sier, STOP!" The sound of his mother's voice halted the blow in mid-air. "Please..."

Riva's anguished cry filled the arena as she pleaded with one of her sons for the life of the other.

"Must a mother lose both of her sons at once?" she wailed.

Sier relented. Dropping his hands, he stood up. Turning his back on his brother, Sier slowly exited the arena.

148

The Ceremony of Zhu Fu

CHAPTER 28

A host of Spatians gathered at the home of Caasi and Riva to celebrate the ceremony of Zhù fú. The garden air buzzed with excitement. It was a high honor to attend the presentation of the cup of blessing to Sier, the firstborn of the House of Caasi.

Members of the Royal Council gathered to witness the transfer of the blessing. They stood along the length of a reflecting pool in the center of Riva's eclectic garden.

Caasi and Riva were seated in delicately carved chairs at the far end of the pool. Riva's favorite ivory flowers bloomed in profusion near the house, and fresh cuttings and boughs of greenery tied with silk adorned the windows facing the garden. The sound of soft music, quiet conversation, and the crisp, exotic scent of the flowers filled the air.

Riva absently twisted her fingers in her lap, and Caasi reached over to squeeze her hands. He looked distracted. His wrinkled brow belied the festive atmosphere of the garden. Caasi had hoped Amo would return home for the ceremony. Despite their shameful brawl and Amo's attempt to steal the honor of Sier's victory at the Dimensional Games, Caasi still prayed for his sons to reconcile. He prayed for there to be peace in his house.

He had delayed long enough. Caasi stood to greet the guests.

"Welcome family and friends of the House of Caasi," he said. "We gather here in the sight of the FINISHER to bear witness to the offering of the cup of Zhù fú." He paused.

"Let the ceremony begin," the Recorders, Palek and Rex, announced in unison. They stepped aside to reveal a kneeling figure clad in dark, flowing robes. The folds of a voluminous hood shrouded the figure's head, obscuring its features.

Seven figures clothed in rags emerged from the rear of the house and carried a pedestal the length of the pool, arms extended above their heads. A worn chalice sat atop the pedestal. The ragged figures and battered chalice contrasted starkly against the festive colors worn by the guests and the brightness of the day. The symbolism was twofold. Together, they represented both the wretchedness of existing without the FINISHER, and the joy of a life lived under his blessing. The chalice bearers paused, carefully lowering the pedestal to the soft ground. A dark red fluid sparkled and sloshed gently in the chalice.

Caasi stepped forward, in front of the kneeling figure.

"Your garments symbolize the dark and shifting mystery of the unknown," he began. "Before the FINISHER, we are like a blank slate, after which he writes his will for our lives. The words of this Zhù fú have been given to me as the permanent script for your life, my son. They represent light shed upon the path you must tread."

Placing his hand upon his son's bowed head, Caasi closed his eyes and, after a moment, began to sway as if in a trance.

"It is the will of the FINISHER to give you abundance without measure. You will be lord over all, and all will bow down to you. Your words will utterly bless, and your curses utterly destroy. All the power and authority given me by the FINISHER will be amplified beyond degree in you," declared Caasi. "Drink the cup and receive the blessing of the FINISHER's will for you."

He drank from one side of the chalice before offering the other to the hooded figure to drink.

When they had both drunk, he said, "It is written, my son! I hereby declare to this assembly that it is yours to sit on the ruling Council of Spatium when I am translated into the very presence of the FINISHER," his eyes now sparkling and alert, Caasi paused, his voice full of emotion, "You will serve as progenitor to the FINISHER's new creation and reign sovereign over the glorious enigma of time as Time-Ruler!"

"These words are light, revealing the path declared for you by the FINISHER himself," declared the twin voices of the Recorders. "Let the celebration of your destiny now begin!"

Caasi stepped forward and removed the ceremonial hood. A sharp intake of breath knifed through the gathering. The son staring back at Caasi, eyes blazing in defiance, was Amo.

∞

Sier burst into the garden to find Amo standing before Caasi and the others. "What is the meaning of this?" His steely gaze quickly took in the tableau. The cup of Zhù fú rested between Caasi and Amo. "I am the first born!" he roared.

"Oh, my son! What have I done? Another has received the cup!" Caasi wailed in anguish.

"That's impossible!" Sier's face reddened, his narrowed eyes darting between anger and disbelief like caged animals. "But, the inheritance is mine!"

He glared at Amo, fists clenching and unclenching as he spoke.

His words came in furious bursts as he addressed Caasi. "Has he not disgraced your name enough—hiding behind a mask like a coward— profaning the honor of the Dimensional Games?"

"It is done." Deflated, Caasi slumped into the ivory chair.

"But, Father, what about me?" Sier demanded.

The guests, mouths agape, stepped backward as Sier advanced toward Caasi, his hands stretched forth, his voice pleading. "Is there not a blessing for me?"

Riva caught Amo's attention. Her eyes begged urgently for him to leave. He slipped behind Caasi and quickly exited the scene from the rear of the garden, dropping the ceremonial robes to the floor as he went.

"My son, my son!" Caasi cried. "What is there for me to do? The blessing of preeminence has been pronounced upon your brother!"

"Deceiver!" Howling, Sier fell to his knees. His accusation reverberated throughout the garden.

∞

Amo raced away from the ceremony and into the shadow of the trees, intent on escaping the sound of his brother's pain and wrath. Even as he ran, a small, prideful smile threatened to curve the corners of his lips.

∞

Deep within the labyrinthine corridors of the Hall of Letters, Amo's mockery soon gave way to heartbreak as he realized the implications of his deceptions. He could never face his father after disgracing him so! Was he at heart indeed a liar and a thief?

And what of Sier? Surely Sier would have him isolated in Containment with no hope of release. Or worse, he would simply dispatch him.

What had he been thinking? His mother had seemed so confident, her premonitions so convicting! Now he was utterly alone, certain that even the FINISHER would abandon him for his treachery.

"Help me! Forgive me!" Amo sobbed. "What have I done?"

Chest heaving, he struggled to keep quiet lest someone hear his cries and find him where he hid in the temple.

"Please, help me make it right!" His breath came in ragged gasps. He prayed to the FINISHER and wept until his hoarse gasping lulled him into a troubled sleep.

∞

A giant loomed ahead of him, unreachable from where Amo stood in semi-darkness, far below. An unbearably bright light shone from the giant's face until a small, dark circle of a mouth began to open until it was impossibly wide, literally turning the entirety of the being's face into a gaping hole.

Without warning, light streamed forth from the orifice toward Amo but stopped just short of obliterating him. Instead, it lit two candles on stands in front of him, one to his left, the other to his right. By their light, he saw two doors in the darkness beneath the bright-faced giant.

Amo watched incarnations of Sier and himself as Fledgling boys emerge from the darkness and take the lighted candles. The child Sier took the leftmost candle and walked toward the door on the left. It opened, and inside, Amo saw a bright, beautifully decorated room full of smiling, playing children. The child with the candle eagerly entered the room, and seeing no need for the light, blew out the candle and tossed it aside.

Next, the child Amo took the remaining candle and walked toward the still-closed door on the right. When he reached it, the door opened to reveal a dark, dreadful room full of crying, dirty children. He held out the candle and walked into the room. Its light filled the space, illuminating the faces of each crying child.

In an instant, the image of the children vanished, and a multitude of people surrounded Amo. Their faces were masks of terror; their anguished cries rang over and over again in his ears before he realized what they were shouting.

"We're out of time!"

A mature Sier's face loomed dispassionately over the masses.

"Sier!" Amo heard his own voice, a plea above the din. "Sier, please, stop this!"

The emotionless Sier cocked his head, his face suddenly widening in a mirthless grin.

"You stop it, TIME-RULER!" he sneered.

Amo felt the swirling mist and the smooth, cold surface of the temple floor against his face.

Revelation

CHAPTER 29

Riva rushed forward to console Sier and to assuage his anger in front of all of their guests. She assured him that everything would work out for the best, though Amo, and not he, had drunk from the cup of Zhù fú and received Caasi's irrevocable blessing.

Hearing her words, Caasi knew that Riva had been Amo's accomplice in stealing the blessing of the firstborn. Now that everyone had gone and they were alone, he found the courage to express his deepest fear to her.

"I was certain that the successor to my house and the sovereign of the FINISHER's new creation would be Sier," Caasi said softly. "We have long battled over which of our sons was ordained to be Time-Ruler, but I see, we have battled over much more."

He lovingly traced the features of his wife's face with his finger as if committing them to memory. "Have I heard rightly, or have you?"

Tenderly, he kissed the top of her head. He set off for the Hall of Letters to pray.

∞

Caasi stepped onto the glowing deck of the Link. He was calmed by its steady hum, much like the soothing song of a living thing. He felt the familiar undulation beneath his feet as the deck rose and fell with a life of its own. The air around him grew misty. It swirled and eddied in pools that formed and dissolved with the wave-like motion of the ground.

Before long, he had traveled farther out onto the bridge where the breeze intensified. The smooth swelling of the luminescent deck steadily increased until it heaved and writhed violently under him. He was in the center of a storm now. The pit of his stomach trembled, recoiling in abject terror, until helpless against the wind, he cried out.

The familiar voice, strong and deep, like the sound of rushing waters, grew steadily in his ears. In an instant, that voice, stronger than the undulating waves and more powerful even than the wind, grew still and small. "Be still," it commanded. And immediately, peace and joy overwhelmed Caasi; pure, blinding light flooded his soul as he stepped into the center of the Link and was translated.

∞

"Wise and gracious FINISHER, I pray you would allow my daughter to awaken, that she might rise to serve you once again. My heart is thankful for the accomplishment of whatever is your will." Spiritus rose from his knees, ending his prayers at Rachel's bedside.

Tears streamed down his cheeks as he held her cold, limp hand in his own. He sat in the chair he had pulled up close to where she lay motionless, under unfathomable depths of sleep. After a moment, he allowed himself to collapse against the cushions of the chair.

"Dearest Rachel," he said, his voice choked with emotion, "I fear all is changing around us and I am filled with foreboding. The second rebellion is at hand. Caduceus grows bolder against the council with Caasi's imminent departure. He would move to restore his house to power, given the slightest opportunity."

Stroking her hair, he gently smoothed it away from her face. He straightened himself, his features tense with resolve.

"Our treaty with the House of Caasi assures your marriage to the Time-Ruler," Spiritus said. "We must be strong, daughter. We must remain allied with the FINISHER, and all will be well."

Spiritus stood and cast a loving glance at the still figure of his daughter. He noted how peaceful she looked and left the room, closing the door softly behind him.

The curtains at Rachel's window parted. A lone figure cleared the windowsill and landed silently on the floor, swiftly crossing the room to tower over her bedside.

∞

"I had to come here to see you," Amo whispered to Rachel's still form. He sat gingerly in the chair recently occupied by her father. "I came to apologize. You must know that I was only trying to save you," he said.

He reached out to take Rachel's hand in his own. The same swell of emotion threatened to overtake him as when they stood together at the Unveiling.

Looking down on her face, so calm and peaceful, Amo suddenly realized he never wanted to be without her. He had always loved Rachel as a friend, but now he resolved to love her and protect her with all of his heart, even if she would never know—even if he had to suffer her marriage to his brother and the treaty between their houses.

"So much has happened since the Unveiling," he whispered. "It seems like everything I do makes things worse between my father and me. I wish you could hear me. I've missed you listening." Amo sighed heavily. "You probably would have talked me out of a few things."

Amo told Rachel's sleeping form about fighting Sier disguised as Mask. He recounted his actions at the ceremony of Zhù fú, and his harrowing escape to the maze of corridors in the temple.

His eyelids drooped heavily. He sat, unable to move as Rachel's room swirled and fell away beneath him.

∞

Rachel's room is replaced by the Hall of Letters, and Amo feels himself floating through the crowd milling about all around him. Revelers are enjoying the festive atmosphere of the Unveiling. Across the great hall, he is astonished to see himself and Rachel standing near the stage. He approaches cautiously, staring open-mouthed as he passes through the gathering unnoticed. The chamber is silent, though he can see people laughing and talking. He knows he should be hearing the sounds of revelry, and yet all around him is eerily quiet. Instinctively he is aware that he is invisible—unseen and unperceived by anyone in the room. He nears the spot where he and Rachel are talking. He remembers the moment and stops in his tracks as his own face turns in his direction, seemingly trying to perceive himself among the crowd. In an instant, the other Amo is facing Rachel again, inviting her to dance with a jerk of his head toward the makeshift dance floor. He watches as Rachel grabs his hand, and the two of them race up the stairs to join the other couples.

He turns his head to watch as Hittitaes, Serena and Melanie descend the stairs from a balcony overlooking the celebration. At the speed of thought, he is at the top of those same stairs, and can just discern the silhouette of his brother against a window in the outer wall of the pyramid.

Fingers of fear tighten around Amo's belly as Sier turns away from the window to look directly in his eyes. *Can Sier see and hear him?*

Sier is angry. His lips began to move, and suddenly Amo realizes that his brother is looking not at him, but through him. Sier must be addressing someone standing behind him, closer to the balustrade, but as he turns to look, to see the person, Amo is instantly back on the lower floor of the Hall of Letters.

With a gut-wrenching lurch, he realizes he is about to witness the accident again. He covers his eyes with his hands, but all the action around him has slowed to a crawl. As though in a dream, everything is moving in slow motion, except him.

He jerks his head upward as a white-hot sphere emerges from the balcony where he left Sier. It floats slowly but steadily through the air toward the massive column near the dance floor. He watches the explosive impact and sees the top of the column splinter and break away. Why is he seeing this? He tries hard to swallow the lump in his throat as he watches his lame attempt to save Rachel.

And then he sees it. A silver, laser-like flash of energy surges from behind him. It splits the room and hits Rachel in the chest just beneath her chin. She is hurled backward in slow motion. Amo knows that in an instant, she will be pinned against the bottom of the pillar. A knot of dread coiling in his stomach, he slowly turns, following the beam to see where it has come from behind him.

"Hittitaes?" He gasps.

∞

Back in Rachel's room, by her bedside, Amo reached out and carefully moved the neck of her gown aside. In the dim light, he can just make out an ugly brand on her chest, just below her throat. He stared open-mouthed, his eyes darting from the bruise, to the ring on the third finger of his right hand, and back. The jeweled image of the tree perfectly matched the purplish wound on Rachel's chest. Both were the mark of his father's house, the emblem of the House of Caasi.

∞

Bowing his head, Amo prayed that the FINISHER would restore Rachel to health. He vowed revenge on his brother and Hittitaes. He bent to tenderly kiss Rachel's forehead.

"Get away from her!" Spiritus thundered from the door of Rachel's room.

Palek and Rex came running up behind him, alerted by his shout at the sight of Amo leaning over Rachel's bedside.

"How dare you accost my daughter in my home!" Spiritus, livid with rage, flew across the room. He attempted to tackle Amo to the floor.

Amo managed to free himself, but not before Palek had blocked the door. Rex came barreling toward him. Reluctantly, Amo pushed Spiritus into the charging Rex, knocking both to the floor. He leaped over the window sill. He'd hardly landed before getting to his feet to run, quickly putting distance between himself and the woman he loved.

Palek and Rex dashed out of the window to give chase. They landed with a thud as Amo disappeared into the trees bordering Spiritus' property.

Amo could hear them crashing through the brush after him.

∞

Trembling, Spiritus fell back into the chair he had practically lived in since the accident at the Unveiling. He'd kept vigil by his daughter's bedside while she lay in this unresponsive state.

"What is it?" Rex hurried to his friend's side.

"The mark," Spiritus whispered, "just beneath the hollow of her throat..."

Palek bent over Rachel's sleeping form. He inhaled sharply at the sight of the dark lesion on her skin. It had been there since the accident, but now it emerged as more than a wound in her flesh.

"What's wrong?" Rex asked.

"The bruise," Palek answered. "It's the mark of Caasi."

Dispatched

CHAPTER 30

"Your younger brother has received the cup of your father's blessing instead of you—" the stranger taunted.

"How could I know my mother and brother would betray me?" Sier cried, interrupting the stranger's harangue. "I don't even know who you are! How do I know you won't betray me as well?"

"Don't allow petty emotion to blind you!" the stranger said. "There is far more at stake here than a ceremonial blessing, but all is not lost."

"I have been declared Time-Ruler!" Sier snorted. "I am heir to my father's seat on the Royal Council of Spatium!"

"Don't behave like an arrogant fool!" the stranger said. "Caasi has pronounced the cup of Zhù fú upon your brother!"

"There is no doubt about my power. No ceremonial cup of drivel can change that!" Sier said.

"In light of your father's blessing, Spiritus will surely consider granting Amo a seat on the Royal Council!" the stranger said.

"Impossible!" Sier said.

"Is it?" the stranger hissed. "Think! Your father is gone. Your brother is on the run. In their absence, you must erase all doubts regarding your leadership of Spatium, or Amo will resurface to challenge you," he said, pausing to let the thought sink in.

"He may even incite the council to question your right to reign—"

"I don't believe you!" Sier shouted, interrupting the stranger and trying to sound more confident than he felt. "Why won't you reveal yourself to me?" he asked. "Maybe then I would find your words more credible."

"Soon enough," the stranger said. "More importantly, Spiritus must not be allowed to seat Amo on the Council."

"I will not harm Spiritus," Sier said, his voice steady.

"No one is asking you to harm him," the stranger said. "But do what you must to obtain the Meta Symbols, or you will remain a slave to Caasi's dreams instead of master of your own. "

"What do you stand to gain by my success?" Sier asked.

"Suffice it to say that I am one who would see the FINISHER's new creation under your rule and Spatium under new enlightenment," the stranger said. His lips curled in a mirthless smile.

∞

Sier hurried to meet Hittitaes in the shadows. The thought of her waiting drove all thoughts from his mind. The threatening words of the stranger, Caasi's departure, and avenging himself against Amo, all fled before the warm invitation of her embrace.

She ran to meet him, and he gathered her in his arms. The tension of his encounter with the white entity drained away.

"I thought you'd forgotten," she breathed, her face against his neck.

"Never! Nothing could keep me from you!" Sier smoothed the length of her dark hair.

"I was worried!" She grasped his hands and stepped away from him, stretching their arms between them.

"Have you been attending to your mother?" Hittitaes tilted her head with the question.

The filigree chain glinted in the dim light. Sier flushed at the thought of his ring at the end of those links, cradled against the softness of her skin.

"Yes," he lied. No need to tell her about his conversation with the stranger and its dire implications, he thought. He dropped her hands, waving his own in a gesture meant to push the returning angry thoughts away. "She is lost without my father," he continued, "but soon, the celebration of his Translation will begin. The festivities will lift her spirits."

"And your brother?" Hittitaes asked.

Sier's brow furrowed in annoyance. "What of him?" he snapped.

She reached for his hand and pressed it against her cheek.

His features softened. "I'm sorry," he said. "Neither my mother nor I have seen Amo since the ceremony. I'm not sure he even knows of my father's departure." Sier's eyes clouded, unshed tears threatening to spill over. He would miss Caasi.

"Sier, love, the departure of Caasi saddens all of Spatium." Hittitaes spoke soothingly, her lips pressed against his fingertips. She moved close in the circle of his embrace. "But surely, we are now free to be together. You needn't be bound to another against your wishes."

Sier inhaled deeply, slowly breathing out the words. "It was my father's wish before his departure that I honor his treaty with Spiritus, and marry Rachel."

He felt her stiffen in his arms. "You can't possibly be thinking of going through with that!" she spat.

"I need to think—"

"About what? You said you loved me!" Hittitaes' eyes bore into him.

"I do, but I also love my father," Sier said. "I cannot lightly abandon the covenant he made with Spiritus. I don't love Rachel. But until she awakens, what can I do?"

"What if she never regains consciousness?" Hittitaes asked. "Would you pledge your loyalty, your fortune, to an inanimate shell? To what purpose?"

Sier didn't answer. The sweetness of their meeting irreparably soured, he walked Hittitaes near to her father's house.

Hittitaes strode along, not caring if anyone saw how angry she was. But she had chosen their meeting place well. They met no one in the stony silence as they traversed the lush grounds of Caduceus' property.

Sier watched as she entered a door at the back of the house. When she was indoors, he turned to leave.

Once she was certain he wouldn't look back and see her, Hittitaes slipped outside. Carefully and quietly, she followed Sier.

∞

The words of the stranger dogged Sier's thoughts all the way to Spiritus' house, relentlessly echoing in his mind.

"You will remain a slave to Caasi's dreams instead of master of your own," the stranger had said.

Long before he reached Spiritus and Rachel's home, Sier knew what he would do.

∞

"Counselor Spiritus, it's Sier, sir." He waited outside the door to Spiritus and Rachel's home. A cottony mist had settled along the ground, blanketing the grounds and surrounding hillside with fluffy patches of cool dampness. "I've come to see you about Rachel."

Spiritus opened the door. "Hello, son. Come in."

He led Sier through the main floor of the house and out a wall of glass-paneled doors to an expansive patio. "We can visit out here without disturbing Rachel. This was—is—" he corrected himself, "one of her favorite parts of our home."

A profusion of sweet-smelling vines clung to an arbor attached to the house and extending over the patio. Peachy orange blossoms played hide and seek in the mist among the dark green foliage.

"I'm glad you've come, though I'm afraid Rachel's condition remains the same," Spiritus said.

"I'm sorry to hear that," Sier said. He was genuinely sad to hear Rachel had not improved.

They reached a small grouping of garden chairs just beyond the shadows under the arbor. Spiritus sat and motioned for Sier to join him. His eyebrows arched in mild surprise when Sier remained standing.

"With all due respect, Counselor, my visit will most likely not endear me to you." Sier looked Spiritus directly in the eyes, gathering his resolve. "I cannot go through with the covenant my father made with you."

Spiritus inhaled sharply. The intoxicating scent of the flowers belied the sickening lurch of his stomach.

"I will not marry Rachel, when I love someone else." Sier was determined to say everything before giving Spiritus a chance to object. "I plan to marry Hittitaes."

Spiritus had risen from his seat. He now stood, facing Sier.

"Caduceus has brought division on the council," he said, his voice low and intense. If his daughter shares his beliefs, it will surely lead Spatium away from all that your father sought. I urge you, do not wed the daughter of Caduceus!"

"Sir, I love Hittitaes," Sier said. "Nothing will change that. I came here to assure you that I will honor my father's intentions regarding the council, but I will not marry Rachel."

"You say you will honor your father's intentions! Do you even know what they were?" Spiritus asked. He stared into Sier's eyes, his features taut with anger.

"Where he sought to maintain the unity of Spatium, would you tear it apart by your rebellion?" Spiritus asked.

Sier's face remained impassive, his lips set in a firm line. He allowed his eyes to sweep over the graceful shapes of the topiaries clustered off the far end of the patio.

Spiritus tried another tack. "Our families were chosen for a special purpose—to unite Spatium in the face of outright rebellion against the FINISHER. You are Time-Ruler! Your bride will give birth to a people who will be loyal to the FINISHER! They will be the guardians of his new creation. For your own progeny's sake, do not be misguided by your flesh and emotions!"

Spiritus spread his hands imploringly. "Your father feared your lack of zeal for the prophecies would be your downfall and the ruin of Spatium." He sighed heavily, resigned to the uncaring look on Sier's face.

Certain further attempts to sway Sier with words would have no effect, the Counselor became silent. He thought for a long moment, his eyes widening suddenly in revelation.

"Oh, my!" he sighed. "Amo—he has powers to rival your own!" He tore at the fabric of his tunic, pacing back and forth across the tiled patio. "FINISHER, forgive us! Have we been wrong?" he wailed, seemingly oblivious to Sier's presence. "Was Caasi misguided, blinded by favoritism?"

Counselor Spiritus did not ponder the question for long. Instead, he collected himself and nodded resolutely. "The Royal Council must reconvene. We must reconsider the prophecy and the identity of Time-Ruler!"

"That won't be necessary!" Sier quickly strode toward Spiritus, fists clenched. "Just give me the symbol!"

"What are you talking about?" Spiritus' eyes narrowed to slits.

Undaunted, Sier stared back at the Counselor.

"I know about the Meta Symbols," he said. "That they unlock the secrets of the book of Fabula and Syuzhet!" He took a menacing step toward Spiritus.

"And I know you have one of them! Give it to me!" Sier's eyes were wild. He was tired of playing games.

"You know nothing!" Spiritus scoffed.

Sier was startled to see the luminous being appear beneath the arbor, nearly hidden amidst the shrubs and heavy mist that clung to the house.

"I would do as he says, if I were you," the being said to Spiritus.

Spiritus whirled to face the intruder. "What are you doing here?" he demanded.

Sier raised his eyebrows in surprise. Counselor Spiritus seemed to recognize the glowing creature.

"You evil snake!" Spiritus fumed, raising a fist toward the white entity.

Returning his attention to Sier, Counselor Spiritus raised his voice to thunder, "How dare you pretend to honor your father's legacy, when all the while you're conspiring with this usurper!" He railed, pointing at the creature. Then he rushed toward Sier, his hands claw-like, his face a seething mask of rage. "You are unworthy to bear the name Caasi!"

All at once, Spiritus stood frozen. Slowly, the muscles of his face relaxed, the heat of his emotions drained away. He fell forward into Sier's arms.

Sier's eyes widened in shock. His hands trembled as he lowered Spiritus' injured body to the tiled patio floor.

"What have I done?" The terrified question came, causing Sier to look up.

"Hittitaes?" Sier stared in disbelief as Hittitaes emerged from the topiary garden, suddenly rushing toward him.

Hittitaes fell to her knees in the mist beside Spiritus. She bent to shake him, as if to revive him from sleep. The rich auburn of her hair fell across Spiritus' face, a flood of dark crimson against the pallor of the dispatched council member's skin.

"I'm sorry!" Hittitaes wailed. "I'm so sorry! I followed you. I saw the two of you arguing."

Her voice rising, she frantically twisted the fabric of Spiritus' linen tunic in her hands.

"He said those awful things! How could he threaten to take his ridiculous speculations to the Royal Council?"

She thrust the fabric away and stood, clutching desperately at Sier's arm. "He would make Amo Time-Ruler instead of you!" she shrieked. "I thought Spiritus would dispatch you, Sier!"

Sier pulled away, closing his eyes and grasping the sides of his head. His thoughts swam about in a frenzy. "I don't know what to do," he said slowly. "Will I have to bring you before the Royal Council?" His voice broke with sorrow.

Hittitaes crumpled to the ground. She buried her face in her hands, muting her pitiful sobs.

"Do you really want to do that, Sier?" A disembodied voice came from beneath the arbor.

Hittitaes lifted her head and peered into the shadows at a glowing shape near the house.

"I have no choice," came Sier's disheartened reply.

"Who is that?" Hittitaes whispered.

"It seems to me that you're just as guilty as she is." Ignoring her question, the glowing being continued to address Sier.

"How dare you accuse me! I'll dispatch you myself!" Sier bellowed, though he didn't move from where he stood near the body of Spiritus.

"It's a horrible thing to have dispatched one Spatium council member," the being said. "The punishment would be inconceivable if you were to dispatch two."

"What! What are you talking about?" Sier shouted. "I am not responsible for this!"

"His wound bears the mark of the House of Caasi," the being said.

Sier bent to look. An ugly mark scorched Spiritus' flesh. He gasped at the sight of his family's signet emblazoned on the side of Spiritus' head.

"My ring." Sier's voice faltered, fading to a whisper. "Why would you do this to me?" He turned to look down at Hittitaes.

"I wanted to help you. I didn't mean to..." Tears spilled from her slate-gray eyes.

The brilliant entity stepped forward from the shadows of the arbor. His movement drew Sier's and Hittitaes' attention as he revealed his face.

"Caduceus!" Sier shouted.

"Father!" Hittitaes whispered.

Caduceus gestured toward the motionless form of Spiritus, ignoring their outcries. "Swear your allegiance to me, or you will suffer," he said. "It is your mark upon Spiritus. No one will believe you did not dispatch him."

Caduceus' voice took on a lilting, conciliatory tone. "Your father has gone. No more tests to prove you're worthy. It's clear your mother loved Amo and not you. She helped him steal your inheritance, under your father's nose!" he taunted. "Be wiser than Caasi ever was! Choose now your destiny with the woman you love, or your ruin!"

Enraged, hot tears streaming down his cheeks, Sier hurled himself forward to attack Caduceus.

"Wait!" Hittitaes screamed. "Sier, my love! I'm so sorry for what I've done!" she sobbed. "I love you more than anything, but if you destroy my father, you will destroy me, too." Her tears flowing freely, she pleaded with Sier to abandon his rage and side with Caduceus.

∞

Palek and Rex lost track of Amo in the woods. They returned to the house to find Counselor Spiritus barely alive where he lay on the patio outside.

"May the FINISHER help us!" Rex hurried over to Spiritus and knelt beside him.

"What's happened?" Palek cried.

"I can't tell, but he's very weak." Rex gently searched for signs of injury. "I'm not sure there's much we can—Oh, no!" He cried.

"What is it? What's the matter?" asked Palek.

Rex gingerly turned Spiritus' head to one side. The purplish-black imprint of a tree was clearly visible. Its bare branches were scorched into Counselor Spiritus' skin. His lifeless body began to glow.

"There's nothing we can do for him, now," Rex said.

He and Palek knelt. They closed their eyes and bowed their heads to pray as they waited for Spiritus' body to be taken into the light.

Suddenly a rush of wind exited Spiritus' mouth, tore up the side of the house, and entered a second-story window. The light intensified until, in a flash, the body of Spiritus was gone.

∞

Rachel was lifted bodily and lay suspended, levitating above her bed. A gust of wind surged through the open window and filled the room. She sat up in mid-air, fully awake, eyes wide with terror, her hair swirling about her.

"Father?" she whispered. "Father!"

Suddenly, she knew, and the knowledge stabbed like the sharpest knife. In that instant, the rushing wind was gone. The room went dead calm, and she landed on the bed with a thud.

Her grief-stricken sobs brought Palek and Rex rushing upstairs from outside.

Rise of Caduceus

CHAPTER 31

Palek and Rex stood before the assembled members of the Royal Council of Spatium and reported the dispatchment of Counselor Spiritus. A collective gasp was heard throughout the chamber.

Malaika and Tomos, along with Albar, Captain of the Protectorate, immediately rose to their feet.

"Who would dare!" shouted Malaika.

Tears sprang to Daphne's eyes. Caden and Tomos comforted her, even as they strained forward to hear more of Palek and Rex's report.

"Please, everyone remain calm," Sophia admonished.

Palek and Rex recounted how they'd witnessed an argument between Counselor Spiritus and Amo at the Counselor's home, and that they had gone in pursuit of Amo when he ran off. Unable to find him, they returned to discover the Counselor fatally wounded, lying on the patio outside.

"Amo must have doubled back," said Palek.

"Or perhaps he never left, waiting to confront Counselor Spiritus after we went out looking for him," Rex offered. His voice was tinged with unfathomable regret.

The council members sat in stunned silence.

Caduceus rose to speak first. "We Spatians are people who grow closer and stronger in adversity. I believe this is an opportunity to manifest those attributes."

Instructor Em Sartor and Caden, along with several other council members nodded in agreement.

"Leaders like Caasi and Spiritus are impossible to equal," Caduceus went on, "so, let that not be our ambition! Instead, let our goal be to exceed even their successes! This crisis calls for a leader with foresight beyond even that of the renowned Caasi and Spiritus. My dear departed brothers often objected to my vision for the leadership of Spatium. Our many clashes in your midst are well documented. He would tell you if he could, our battles were for the good of Spatium. Is it not written that iron sharpens iron? I tell you that I'm indeed sharper for his friendship."

"It is no secret you opposed Caasi's vision for the leadership of Spatium," Tomos countered. "You do well to honor his legacy, but is this esteemed council to believe you would now choose to support him?" he leaned forward, his expression openly challenging.

Malaika said, "Certainly no one here relishes Caasi's absence more than you, Caduceus."

"I respect Caasi's legacy," Caduceus addressed Tomos, then directed his gaze toward Malaika. "I, too, will miss his overwhelming presence. But we all must admit he appears to have lacked judgment leading up to his departure. His own household is divided amongst his sons. One is a respected warrior and ruler, and the other a liar and a fugitive. It is clear that Caasi's reliance on a mythical FINISHER and a tired book of mirrors did nothing to keep peace in his own home."

"Careful, brother," warned Caden. "It was Caasi who spearheaded your reinstatement to the council following the rebellion wherein a third of your house was lost!"

"For which, no doubt, I will forever be his debt," Caduceus said. "However, in light of Caasi's misfortunes and the unforeseen dispatchment of dear Spiritus, perhaps it is no longer wise to heed the dictates of an invisible deity issuing indecipherable prophecies."

"This is a mockery!" Sophia said. "I, for one, will not tolerate your insolence! How dare you speak of the FINISHER and his servant Caasi in such a manner?"

"I beg a thousand pardons if my opinion offends you, wise Sophia," said Caduceus. "As a matter of fact, in the spirit of unity, I hereby welcome and affirm Sier Caasi as Spatium's newest council member!"

As though on cue, Sier entered the chamber from without the sanctuary doors. He strode in and stood behind Caasi's empty seat at the table.

The council members, surprised by Caduceus' endorsement of Sier, tentatively began clapping.

"Take your seat, my son," said Caduceus. He bowed with a flourish. "Sier is to be Time-Ruler of the FINISHER's new creation. He will also assume his father's seat on the council, per Caasi's last officially recorded wishes. If there are any objections, let them be spoken now."

"I will not sit idly by while you assume authority over this council, Caduceus!" Sophia challenged. "Would you appoint yourself a leader without an election?"

"Fair enough!" said Caduceus, "I believe the venerable Sophia has moved for a fair election of the successor to Caasi as leader of this council by customary vote. I hereby second that motion, and submit myself as candidate."

"Moved," said Palek.

"And seconded," said Rex.

"Am I to run unopposed, or may I have the honor of you as my opponent, Sophia?" Caduceus asked.

"You may, indeed," Sophia said. She fixed her sharp eyes on Caduceus in an unflinching stare.

"Moved and seconded," announced Palek and Rex.

Palek produced the scrolls, on which each council member inscribed his or her name and the name of Sophia or Caduceus.

Rex received the scrolls as each council member came forward to cast a ballot. As official Recorders, he and Palek would not vote.

When the last council member had recorded his vote, Rex signaled they were ready to declare the outcome.

Palek and Rex began the announcement in unison.

"The election to replace Caasi as leader of the Royal Council of Spatium yields the following results...

For Caduceus—Albar.

For Caduceus—Daphne.

For Sophia—Tomos.

For Caduceus—Em Sartor.

For Sophia—Malaika.

For Sophia—Caden."

The chamber fell silent. Sier's vote would break the tie and establish his allegiances on the council.

Palek and Rex continued, "For Caduceus—Sier."

Sophia glared defiantly at Caduceus. He returned her stare, even as the other council members breathed an uneasy sigh or hung their heads.

Sier had helped Caduceus' second rebellion to succeed, but not without opposition. The battle lines were now firmly drawn between Caduceus and Sophia.

"Esteemed council members," announced Recorders Palek and Rex simultaneously, "by virtue and integrity of your signatures upon these scrolls, you have elected to install Caduceus successor to the venerable Caasi and leader of the Royal Council of Spatium."

Caduceus spoke, his voice piercing the air like a dagger. "If there is nothing to be heard in defense of Amo Caasi, I hereby order that he be seized and detained acts of theft and deception to be enumerated hereafter, and for the dispatchment of our highly exalted brother, Spiritus!"

Albar, Captain of the Protectorate, nodded and excused himself from the assembly. He set off to rally the forces of the temple guard under his command to capture Amo Caasi.

As he exited the chamber, the voices of Palek and Rex spoke in unison behind him. "These are the first official recorded acts of..."

"Caduceus, successor to Caasi," said Palek.

"and leader of the Royal Council of Spatium," said Rex.

∞

"Mother, I'm sorry about all that has happened, but I will not marry Rachel," said Sier. "My heart is with Hittitaes."

"Then you are a fool, my son," Riva said with finality.

"I'm sorry you feel that way. I no longer care what you think of me," Sier spat the words. "It doesn't even matter that you have always preferred Amo over me!"

"How dare you speak to me in this manner!" Riva shouted. "Your father would have had you dispatched for your insolence!"

"My father? Ha!" Sier scoffed.

The lion's mane of Sier's hair made him look larger and more imposing than Riva had ever seen him. She trembled involuntarily as Sier's eyes narrowed to slits and seemed to bore through her. She suddenly knew he sensed her unease.

Sier jerked his head to one side like a predator catching the sharp scent of fear off its prey.

"My father is departed," he said. "And, in my eyes, so is my mother. Who is father or mother to me? From now on, the members of my family are those who do my will."

∞

Riva slipped inside Caasi's study and locked the door behind her. She drew the heavy draperies closed before hurrying across the room. She stopped in front of the floor-to-ceiling wall of books opposite Caasi's massive desk. She brushed away the tears threatening to spill from her eyes.

"Amo? Amo, it's me," she said. She waited before the wall of books, her face resolute despite her tears. She was determined to warn Amo of Sier's plans.

A segment of the shelving melted away to reveal the contents of a medium-sized room. The drone of an electrified field warned her not to proceed. Amo reached a panel near the door, and the field dissipated, allowing Riva to enter.

Amo clicked the energy field back on, and the panel of shelving reappeared in its place. Caasi's study could be seen on the other side, but anyone looking in the direction of the hidden room would only see the hologram of the wall of books.

Mother and son fell into each other's arms, overwhelmed with a mixture of joy and grief.

"Oh, my dear!" Riva cried. "You are so much like your father. How I miss him!" Riva wiped at fresh tears.

Amo felt mixed emotions over the translation of his father. The loss saddened him. The absence of Caasi's presence was felt throughout Spatium. But soon enough, the period of mourning would give way to a celebration of Caasi's translation into the rapturous presence of the FINISHER.

"I must tell you that your brother has vowed revenge." Riva interrupted Amo's thoughts, eager to tell him of Sier's plans. "He will seek you here, before long."

She wrung her hands. "If he discovers you here after the mourning, he may not hesitate to dispatch you."

Her upraised hand silenced his objection.

"At least in the temple, you will be safe from such an attempt!" she said. "My only concern now, my son, is for your life and the life of your brother."

Amo nodded reluctantly. He knew that to lose both sons, one dispatched at the other's hand, would be more than she could bear, especially without Caasi. He also knew that her heart's desire now would be to join him.

"Know also that he plans to marry Hittitaes," Riva said gravely.

Amo was stunned. His thoughts came in rapid succession. Caasi was beloved by all of Spatium. Surely the people would not follow Sier if he abandoned his father's wishes and wed Hittitaes. What about Rachel?

∞

In the sanctuary of the Hall of Letters, Amo knelt to pray. He had taken his mother's advice and run to the only place he felt he might find refuge until he could figure out how to protect Rachel, and what to do about Sier.

"Oh, great FINISHER, I need you now more than ever," he prayed. "I feel so lost and alone. My father is gone, and I've left my mother. My brother seeks my life and maybe that of my—" he couldn't finish the thought. He wanted Rachel to be much more to him than a friend. Would he ever get the chance to tell her so?

"My father used to say the answers are not in our mind, but in your book," he continued. "Well, I don't understand! Why did you make me a son of Caasi? Am I a mistake? Or an afterthought? What are you doing? I feel like I'm caught inside of a story you've already written, and it's all right here!"

Amo rushed over to where the book of Fabula and Syuzhet rested on its pedestal. He threw open its cover. His own reflection stared back at him from the silvery pages. "It's right here, but I don't see it!" He pounded his fist against the book. Instantly his reflection dissolved, and a tremor shook the temple from floor to ceiling. Amo stood, rooted to the spot. A group of letters formed above the pages of the book.

∞

"Wake up. Wake up, dear," coaxed Sophia. She knelt where Amo lay on the temple floor and gently shook his arm.

"I, I was praying," Amo said. "I must have fallen asleep." He rubbed at his eyes with both fists and sat up.

"I understand, my dear," Sophia said. "There is no better rest than that found in the arms of the FINISHER." She nodded, the hint of a smile shaping her lips. "Why are you running?" she asked.

"I'm not running," Amo lied. The memory of why he happened to be asleep on the temple floor came rushing back, overwhelming him with fear and sadness.

"I never said you were running away from anything." Sophia's voice was calm and soothing.

Amo thought she was taller than most of the men he knew. She cut an imposing figure, even as she knelt beside him. He peered through the dim light to search her face and was comforted by the softness of her features.

"Some people simply run away from trials they don't understand," Sophia said. "Others run to them. Which is it for you?"

"I'm afraid I don't understand," Amo said.

"You will," said Sophia, "For now, you must go. The other council members are arriving, and I fear Caduceus will not honor the rule of sanctuary. He may be conspiring with Sier to take your life." She paused. "Without Caasi or Spiritus, I will not be able to protect you."

"But why? What has happened to Spiritus?" Amo asked.

"Spiritus has been dispatched." Tears filled Sophia's eyes and spilled down her cheeks, but her voice remained steady and calm.

"He, your father, and I were the only members willing to stand firm in our loyalty to the FINISHER and the prophecies," she said. "With both of them gone, I'm afraid I will be hard-pressed to thwart Caduceus' efforts to sway the council members to his side."

"But who would dare do that?" Amo sputtered, overcome with disbelief. A small knot of fear took hold in his belly.

"Caduceus has convinced the council that you are the culprit," Sophia said.

Amo's fear gave way to panic. "What? Why would anyone accuse me of such a thing?" His eyes anxiously searched her face, while his heart hammered in his chest.

"You must go now!" Sophia's features grew taught, and her voice was firm. "Caduceus' allies are on their way! Sier can't be far behind!"

"But I have nowhere to go!" Amo cried.

"Here, come quickly!" she urged. She led him to a rear door of the sanctuary and pushed him from the room. "Make your way to the main corridor. You will find help there."

In the dim light, Amo hurried along the corridor, unsure of where it led. It didn't matter. He was desperate to escape his brother's and Caduceus' mob.

The Lines Are Drawn

CHAPTER 32

Riva struggled to stifle a gasp at the sight of Rachel. She hurriedly opened the door to the weakened wisp of a girl on the other side. Riva swept the forlorn figure into her arms in a motherly embrace. They stood there for a long moment, sharing their grief in quiet sobs.

"Come, you must tell me all that has happened." Riva put an arm around Rachel and gently led her down the long hall toward the family room and beyond to Caasi's study. Though the house was silent, for Rachel, it was alive with the ghosts of happy moments spent here with her parents and the Caasi family. She was grateful for Riva's comforting presence. She let the peace of her memories wash over her.

They entered Caasi's study, and Riva closed the door softly behind them. Rachel had been in this room on only a few occasions that she could remember. When she and other friends were invited to come over to play with Sier and Amo, this room had been strictly off limits as Caasi's sanctuary. The presence of the patriarch of the House of Caasi was strong in the room.

Once in a while, when she was little, she would wander in amidst the tangle of her father's knees and sit on his lap while he waited to meet with Caasi. Riva would bring them a hot drink and run off to fetch the boys. The memory seemed to call her from another world, like a happy experience fighting to keep its place in her tortured mind. Fresh tears spilled onto her cheeks.

Riva quickly crossed the room to a wall lined with shelves of books. Extending a hand to touch one of the volumes lightly, she heard Rachel's sharp intake of breath as the books melted away to reveal the room on the other side. She ushered Rachel inside and resealed the holographic door behind them.

A fire blazed brightly in a small hearth, where a kettle hung over the dancing flames. Riva motioned for the girl to sit beside her on an amply cushioned sofa. She mysteriously produced two mugs and poured them each a draught of steaming, frothy liquid.

Rachel marveled for a moment at the flora and fauna of Spatium, woven into a rich tufted rug at their feet. Riva noticed Rachel's eyes wide with curiosity as she took in the rest of the room.

"This cubbyhole was my husband's sanctuary," she smiled. "We often laughed that you children were so in awe of the other that you never imagined this one existed." The corners of her eyes crinkled at the memory. "Even now, only Amo and I know it's here."

"This was Caasi's sanctuary?" Rachel breathed. Her fingers absently traced the deep stitching on the arm of the sofa. The room was sparsely furnished, just a table flanked by two chairs shared the space with the couch. The well-worn kettle and a couple more mugs completed the furnishings, as far as Rachel could tell. The room was inviting and comfortable, though nothing like the opulent splendor of the rest of the house.

"Caasi would escape to this room when he needed to be alone to pray or study." Riva sighed heavily, tears welling up in her eyes.

Suddenly Rachel caught hold of Riva's words.

"Caasi was...?" She couldn't finish the thought. The question stuck in her throat.

"Yes, dear," Riva patted her hand. "Caasi is translated. The mourning period has not yet passed, but soon enough, we will host the celebration ceremony."

She looked deeply into Rachel's eyes. "I'm so glad you will be here with us. Your family meant so much to Caasi and me, to all of us." She halted, not sure how Rachel had come to be awake and seemingly well, despite her grief-swollen eyes and exhausted appearance.

"Then praise be to the FINISHER for his wisdom in translating your beloved Caasi. We all loved him, Riva," she said. Her eyes misted over, reddened, but sincere.

Riva softly nodded her thanks. Did Rachel know about Spiritus? Riva wondered. She must. Rachel's next words settled her uncertainty.

"My father..." she faltered, then cleared her throat and continued. "My father was not given that privilege." She sat up as straight as she could in the large cushions of the sofa. She pressed her lips together to stop them quivering. "I know the FINISHER is all-wise. Perhaps there is to be some honor in my father Spiritus' dispatchment?"

"Oh, child!" Riva gathered Rachel in her arms and smoothed her hair. A fresh torrent of sobs wracked the younger woman's body even as she sought to stifle them.

Riva patted and soothed. "Your father was a great man, and a wise and beloved teacher. The circumstances of his dispatchment must surely come to light. He will be avenged," she said, taking Rachel's chin in her hand and looking into her tearstreaked face. "You must live on and honor him in the legacy he's left you—"

"Yes!" Rachel's face brightened in surprised recollection. She swept the tears from her face with the back of a hand. "I will honor my father's memory by fulfilling the treaty he made with Caasi!"

She sniffed and stood, her mind furiously working on this distraction from their shared grief.

She would indeed forget her feelings for Amo and commit herself to a covenant with Sier. She would honor her father's memory! "You will help me plan the ceremony, won't you?" she entreated Riva. "I would love—"

"Rachel, poor, dear, Rachel!" The depth of sadness in Riva's voice arrested Rachel where she stood.

Riva resented Sier's reckless behavior. The torrent of his infidelity would wash away this innocent girl's hope of living to honor her father's memory. She bristled at being used as the conduit through which that flood would come.

"I'm afraid where you have chosen to honor your father's memory by adhering to the covenant," Riva said in measured tones, "Sier has not." Riva watched the hopeful light in Rachel's eyes flicker and die.

"I don't understand," Rachel said. "Have I offended Sier in some way?"

"No, no dear, you are in no way at fault—" Riva began.

"Then what? Why would Sier choose to defy his own father's wishes?" Rachel asked.

"Rachel, Sier has decided that he is in love with Hittitaes," Riva said. "He plans to wed her, regardless of Caasi's and Spiritus' expectations."

Rachel's face contorted in surprise, then crumpled in despair.

Riva felt a surge of pity for the girl. Perhaps she had been better off in the shadowy, twilit sleep of her injuries. Instead, Rachel had awakened to a nightmare.

∞

Outside the Hall of Letters, the whole of Spatium gathered to hear the shocking news. The gathering of mourners stretched back along the road from the temple arch to the ramp leading to the Link. Thick, white fog rose from the ground and swirled about them. The overflow of Spatians who didn't fit on the temple side of the Link stood patiently on the opposite bank.

Caduceus occupied a podium facing the assembly, while Sier and the Royal Council of Spatium stood behind him. Sophia and Riva each placed a comforting arm around Rachel. A phalanx of Protectors flanked the entire group. The arch of the Hall of Letters rose majestically in the rear, framing the open entrance to the temple.

"My fellow Spatian citizens," Caduceus allowed his voice to quaver, and the electric hum of his being reverberated through the crowd like a haunting dirge. "Our hearts are broken over the senseless loss of our great Counselor and friend."

Grief-stricken sobs rose on the air. Dispatchment was unnatural, and Spatium's response to it was profound lament.

Caduceus turned slightly left to acknowledge Rachel, softening the lines of his mouth in a contrived look of empathy. "Dearest Rachel," he crooned, "we are honored to have you back in our midst—"

Encouraging words and sympathetic cheers went up from the assembly, interrupting his speech. Caduceus was quiet, permitting the onlookers this spontaneous outpouring of love. "Though we grieve with you in the loss of your father," he continued, "we hold on to the hope that lives in you, his cherished daughter."

Rachel nodded her thanks to the Spatians blanketing the ground as far as she could see. Tears sprang to her eyes and spilled down her cheeks. She wiped them away.

A wave of applause saluted her courage.

Caduceus surveyed the gathering of mourners. He had broken the news of Spiritus' dispatchment and allowed them to express their sympathies for his wretch of a daughter. Now he continued, intent on fanning the flames of their emotions, he would stoke the embers of their disheartened grief to an inferno of bloodthirsty outrage.

"The eclipsing of life is never rational," he said, "and on this sorrowful occasion, especially, we seek to make sense of such a deliberately vile act." He spoke the next words with intensity, pounding the lectern and leaning forward to incite the crowd. "As to motive, it appears the culprit attempted to deceive Spiritus and was caught in the lie!"

Angry whispers, like a surge of heat, swept through the assembly.

∞

Inside the temple, Amo skidded to a halt. His heart trip-hammered in his chest, and his mouth opened and closed wordlessly. Flashes of raw energy arced around a terrifying figure, which loomed ahead, blocking his passage through the corridor. Its entire body was ablaze, yet there it stood, its burning eyes glued to Amo's face. Caasi had told him of the mysterious Torch, the burning ones who stood in the presence of the FINISHER. With all his heart, he wanted to turn and run; instead, Amo fell to his knees and bowed his face toward the floor.

"Fear not," the Torch said, though its lips had not moved.

Amo perceived and understood the words with his soul. "I can't find my way out," he stammered. "Can you help me?"

"Be encouraged!" came the answer. "I am sent by the FINISHER," the Torch said.

Amo followed as the Torch led him to the doors of the outer sanctuary. When they reached the temple arch, it vanished. Amo couldn't see what went on, but he shuddered at the cacophony outside.

∞

Caduceus recounted the list of charges against the accused, careful to avoid naming him until the last possible moment.

"Not only did Spiritus' murderer commit this abhorrent act," Caduceus said, "but he has also stolen temple artifacts …allegedly."

The deafening roar of the crowd drowned out Caduceus' well-placed disclaimer. Then, individual voices rang out, demanding justice.

"Sacrilege!"

"Never has such a thing been done in Spatium!"

"Bring the perpetrator forth to justice!"

"Soon enough!" Caduceus countered.

Its appetite for vengeance whetted, the citizenry grew eager to avenge every crime, real or imagined, committed against its beloved Spiritus.

"Rachel Spiritus' assailant, and the murderer of her father, our venerable Counselor…" Caduceus affected a long pause until the whole of the assembly fairly panted with anticipation. "…is Amo

Caasi!" he shouted. The crowd went silent, and Caduceus allowed the impact of his words to carry across the divide, settling into every soul present.

Suddenly, pandemonium erupted, and the citizens of Spatium exploded with apoplectic shouts of denial.

"We demand proof," they raged.

"Be warned, Caduceus!" Riva cried, stepping out from in front of the Royal Council. "You will suffer for your lies!"

"You need not believe my words at all!" Caduceus sneered. He summoned Palek and Rex forward. "Please, trusted Recorders of the Royal Council of Spatium, relate to this gathering the events you witnessed in the home of our beloved Spiritus, just before his dispatchment."

Palek and Rex recounted the argument and the ensuing fight. They described leaving Spiritus' home in pursuit of Amo.

"We couldn't find him, so we went back to Spiritus' house," Rex said. He paused to dab at his eyes. "When we got there, we found him. He was unconscious." He cleared his throat and continued, "It was already too late. We could do nothing to save him—"

"Amo must have made his way back while we were out searching!" Palek's face clouded over. "Who knows? He may never have left! He may have watched us go, and then attacked Counselor Spiritus while he was alone!" he said.

"You seem terribly certain that Amo Caasi dispatched counselor Spiritus—" Caduceus continued,

"Yes," confirmed Rex.

"Yes, absolutely!" added Palek.

"Why is that?" Caduceus asked. "Why are you so certain of the killer's identity?"

"Because..." Rex hesitated, shaking his head in disbelief. He still could not fathom how such a thing could be. "I was searching for the cause of Counselor Spiritus' condition, looking for some injury that perhaps we could treat—"

"And we discovered the fatal wound, a searing blow to the head, evidenced by the mark of the House of Caasi, charred into his skin!" Palek finished the description of the injury.

Silence fell like a pall over the crowd.

"Then we heard Rachel screaming and rushed upstairs," said Rex.

"For all we knew, Amo could have still been in the house, determined to dispatch her as well!" Palek added.

"Thank you, most honorable council members," Caduceus said. He returned his attention to Rachel, where she stood between Riva and Sophia.

"And now, dear Rachel Spiritus," he said, his eyes widening into enormous black discs, "Is this true?"

"Yes, as far as—" Rachel began.

"Indeed!" Caduceus bellowed, "Spiritus died defending his beloved daughter, who also bears the mark of her assailant!"

The crowd murmured its surprise.

"It pains me to require this of you, dear Rachel," Caduceus said, "but please reveal the mark of your injury, emblazoned upon your flesh!"

Rachel stood, her eyes gashes of fury in an otherwise stoic face. Jaw set, she squared her shoulders and ignored Caduceus' command. Instead, she glared defiantly at him.

"Why would you hesitate to reveal the identity of your attacker?" Caduceus taunted. "No matter. Guards!" He motioned to Raze and Dub, now in the company of the Spatian guard. They seized Rachel by her arms and dragged her to the front of the platform. The crowd roared its disapproval.

"Caduceus!" Sophia shouted above the din, "You overstep your bounds! How dare you treat the daughter of Spiritus in this way!"

Malaika and Tomos stepped forward.

"Release her!" growled Malaika.

"Or, I will see that you do!" Tomos' anger flashed dangerously, his features as sharp as twin blades of a double-edged sword.

Caduceus held up his hand, silencing the council members and the crowd. "I have reason to believe Rachel's allegiance may not have been wholly to her father, or to the treaty he established with Caasi," he shouted, his voice booming in the silence.

Ignoring Sophia and the others, he directed his question to Rachel. "Will you reveal the evidence willingly?" His question met with Rachel's stony gaze. "Very well." Caduceus waved a hand dismissively in her direction.

Without warning, Tilac lunged toward Rachel and callously tore away the fabric of her outer garment. A collective gasp rippled through the crowd.

Rachel's skin crawled, both from Tilac's touch and from the cool air rustling the sheath of her underclothing. The mark of the House of Caasi blemished the skin of her chest, just beneath her collar.

Its purplish blistering had healed into faintly glowing scar tissue, a permanent reminder of her injury, and of her attacker.

"Riva! Venerable wife of our dear departed Caasi," Caduceus continued, his lips curved in contempt, "tell this assembly what mark of injury is seared into the flesh of Rachel Spiritus!"

Riva could see the whitish scar from where she stood. Suddenly the faces of the council members seemed to swirl about her. Her lungs were a vacuum, and she put forth a hand to steady herself. Nearly swooning, she struggled to stay on her feet.

"It is the mark of my husband's house," Riva whispered. "It is the mark of the House of Caasi!"

Battle for Time

CHAPTER 33

"**I** AM INNOCENT!" Amo rushed from the shadows of the temple and onto the platform. Gasps of surprise and rage rippled through the crowd. Malaika and Tomos blocked the guards who stepped forward to seize Amo. He pushed past the council members to stand before Caduceus.

"He's come forward!" Malaika shouted. "Let Amo defend himself!" He raised his shield, threatening to use it against any of the guards who would not yield.

"He has a right to face his accusers!" Tomos said. His sword flashed, menacingly.

"By all means!" Caduceus intoned. "Let Amo Caasi answer the charges against him before this assembly, if he so chooses!"

"I so choose!" Amo stood before Caduceus, trembling with rage.

"Very well, then!" Caduceus said, alternately facing the council and the crowd.

"You are all witness to Amo Caasi's decision! He will answer before you questions pertaining to his actions in the dispatchment of Counselor Spiritus and the attack on his daughter, Rachel, Caduceus said, waving a hand in her direction.

"Answers satisfactorily establishing his innocence shall result in his going free, " he said. "Should his answers prove insufficient to absolve him of guilt, there will be no further trial. He will be summarily dispatched for his crimes."

"Amo Caasi's request to forego a formal trial before the Royal Council of Spatium..." announced the Recorders, Palek, and Rex in unison.

"To determine his guilt or innocence in the dispatchment of Counselor Spiritus..." continued Palek.

"And the attack on his daughter, Rachel Spiritus..." added Rex.

"Is hereby acknowledged..." said Palek.

"And approved," said Rex.

"Let the inquisition begin," they said, together.

As leader of the Royal Council and impartial representative of the citizens of Spatium, Caduceus proceeded to question Amo. "Did you sneak into Rachel's room without her father Spiritus' knowledge?"

"Yes... no, wait, I did go to see Rachel—"

"Were you there to harm her when Spiritus caught and confronted you?" Caduceus asked. "Did you argue with him?"

"Yes, we argued, but no, I wasn't there to hurt anyone," Amo said.

"Why then, did you attack Spiritus and pretend to run off when Palek and Rex tried to stop you?" Caduceus asked.

"I didn't attack Spiritus! I panicked, I ran from his house to the temple for refuge!" Amo said. "I was sure they would dispatch me if they caught me. I had snuck into Rachel's room without her father's permission," he admitted, "but I didn't dispatch Counselor Spiritus! I didn't stay in the house! I ran out, and he was alive." His face brightened. "I ran to the Hall of Letters! Sophia saw me there!"

"Sophia?" Caduceus turned his attention to her. "Was Amo Caasi with you when Spiritus was dispatched?"

"I did see Amo in the temple..." Sophia began. She hesitated, and Caduceus pounced.

"Out with it!" Caduceus demanded.

"Yes, I did see Amo Caasi in the temple, Caduceus!" Sophia shot back. "But he was sleeping when I discovered him. I cannot say when he arrived or how he came to be there."

"Why would I do such a thing?" Amo shouted. "I have no motive for dispatching Spiritus! He was my teacher, a mentor, and my father's friend!"

Caduceus turned to address Riva. "Riva Caasi, did your husband confide to you that Amo had stolen articles from the Hall of Letters?"

"Yes, but—" Riva began.

"And did he tell you that Spiritus suspected Amo of cheating and then lying to him about it?" Caduceus waited for her reply.

Riva looked helplessly at her youngest son. Her eyes never left his face as she answered, "Yes."

Bedlam broke out in the crowd.

"FINISH HIM!"

"His own mother's testimony convicts him!"

"He's as much as confessed!"

Caden, Keeper of the Dimensional Games, interrupted. "There must be some other reasonable explanation for this—"

"The explanation is Amo Caasi's guilt!" Caduceus bellowed.

"That is not true! I am not guilty!" Amo shouted. "I haven't stolen anything. I did not dispatch Counselor Spiritus, and I would never hurt Rachel!"

Suddenly Amo remembered the vision from the Unveiling.

"It was Hittitaes!" he shouted, pointing an accusing finger at

Caduceus' daughter. I saw it all happen!" Amo insisted. "She fired on Rachel at the dance—"

"You have gone too far!" Caduceus shouted. "I will tolerate no more of your appalling, monstrous lies! How dare you accuse my daughter and make this assault on my house! Albar, seize him!"

Captain Albar and several of the Protectorate moved in to secure Amo.

"Let me go! I'm innocent!" he cried, struggling to break free.

More guards closed in. They attempted to restrain him, but with a surge of strength, Amo flung them away like rag dolls.

Albar lunged toward Amo, but he leaped aside. He landed inches from where Hittitaes cowered beside Caduceus on the platform. Panicked, Amo stepped behind her and slipped his arm around her neck. More guards circled and tried to close in.

"Call them off!" Amo yelled.

Hittitaes' terrified gasps barely filled her lungs with air.

"Let her go!" Sier bellowed. "Your battle is with me!"

Amo saw the hatred in Sier's eyes and tightened his grip around Hittitaes' neck. She was losing consciousness, falling almost limp against his chest.

Amo ignored his mother Riva's plea that he think about what he was doing and let the girl go. He heard the voices of council members Tomos and Malaika, urging him to release Hittitaes. Others were saying that if he let her go, everything would be all right.

Caduceus watched the color drain from his daughter's face and cried out, "Enough! Get out of his way!"

Amo eyed the path leading away from the temple. He began backing down it, dragging Hittitaes along. Some of the color returned to her cheeks as he loosened his grip on her airway.

"I'm warning you!" he shouted. "Stay back!"

"Let him through!" Caduceus commanded. The crowd parted and shrank back, giving Amo and Hittitaes a wide berth.

Hittitaes was more awake now. Her cool, almond eyes were wide with fear. They darted from face to face in the crowd.

Sier and the guard advanced steadily but kept their distance.

Once they were well clear of the multitude, Amo shoved Hittitaes forward. He turned and ran while she stumbled and fell to the ground. The guard surged forward but had to slow down to avoid trampling her.

Sier reached Hittitaes first and gathered her in his arms. He pressed her head against his chest.

Caduceus rushed to meet them, snatching Hittitaes from Sier's embrace. "Get him, or you will never lay eyes on my daughter again!" he snarled. "Dispatch him! I don't care if he is your brother!"

Sier roared, clawing his way to his feet to take off in pursuit of Amo.

Hurtling through the brush and up the embankment toward the Link, Amo heard Sier and the mob charging after him. Breath tore through his lungs like fire as he raced over the misty ground.

Ranting, Sier lurched wildly about, steadily closing the distance between himself and Amo. Mere yards away, he heard his brother's labored breathing and could see the sinews of Amo's legs straining in an effort to stay ahead.

Legs pumping furiously, Amo cleared the ramp raced out onto the glowing expanse of the deck. As he neared the middle of the expanse, his heart leaped into his throat. He nearly tumbled to the ground at the sight, rising like a storm cloud in front of him.

Spatians who had gathered on the opposite bank for lack of

room near the Hall of Letters surged up the ramp and onto the Link.

An anxious cry escaped Amo's lips. There was no escape. The blackness of the abyss yawned below. Surely the mob headed across the Link was bloodthirsty enough to dispatch him, he thought.

Somehow he had always known it would come to this. He had no choice but to face down his brother. He whispered a prayer to the FINISHER.

Amo stopped in the center of the bridge and stood, waiting for Sier.

An instant later, Sier emerged from the commotion, backed by Spatium's elite guard.

"Brother!" Sier's voice boomed across the distance between them. He, Albar, and the Protectorate reached the center of the Link just ahead of Caduceus, Hittitaes, and members of the Royal Council, followed by the crowd from in front of the Hall of Letters.

"You have utterly disgraced the House of Caasi!" Sier shouted. "Surrender for your crimes and face the judgment you've earned!"

"Sier, I don't know what is going on, but you know I had nothing to do with any of this!" Amo shouted back. "Before all of Spatium, I declare my innocence! I will not surrender. I would rather be dispatched to the FINISHER here than give up searching for the truth!"

"Then may he give you the grace as you are dispatched!" Sier signaled Albar and his guards to stand down.

Cautiously, the brothers circled each other. They darted and lunged, firing and evading blazing spheres of energy, until frustrated, Sier ran at Amo, overpowering him with brute force.

Sparks of white light flecked Amo's vision as his brother rained blow after blow on his head and upper body. Desperate, he clutched at the sides of Sier's head, his grasping fingers finding purchase on his brother's ears. He simultaneously arched his torso and jerked his arms straight over his head. A sickening thud followed Sier's howl of pain as his momentum carried him forward, sliding his face along the smooth surface of the Link.

Amo flipped Sier's legs over his head, slamming his back into the deck. He dove on top of Sier and pummeled him about the head and neck. Sier rolled forcefully to one side, upsetting Amo's balance and pinning one leg beneath him.

Sier reared back and sent a fist crashing into Amo's nose. His head snapped backward, and now the whole of his vision succumbed to the white spots. Dazed from the first battering, Amo shook his head, unable to discern anything beyond the darting, glittering specks crowding his sight. Sier lifted him by the hair and held him up for everyone to see.

"Let it be known to all of Spatium and the creation to come," he bellowed "I am Amo Caasi's finisher!"

The crowd erupted, wildly cheering their savior.

Riva ran toward her sons, and the crowd fell silent. "Sier! Sier, stop! Please, stop!" she pleaded with one son for the life of the other.

Half turning toward her, Sier halted. "There have been many occasions, Mother, when the sound of your voice prevented me," he said. "You can stop me no longer. I will once and for all be rid of this traitorous liar!"

Sier turned to finish the job, but Rachel rushed forward from behind the guard and attacked him ferociously. She alternately kicked and pummeled him with her fists. She raked the skin of his face with her nails, drawing blood.

Sier tore Rachel's hands from his face and easily swatted her to the ground. Landing with a ghastly thud, Rachel's head struck the surface of the Link. Sightless, her eyes stared into the gray sky until her lids slowly closed over them.

Amo's vision cleared as Rachel hit the deck. Howling with rage, he launched a white-hot fireball that missed Sier's head by a hair.

Twisting, Sier dodged a second blast but was unable to regain his balance to avoid a third. The superheated plasma slammed full force into his mid-section, sending him careening the length of the bridge. He skidded to a halt in front of the mob. Their collective moan buoyed his resolve, though he was doubled over in agony. Each breath brought shards of pain that seared his lungs. Sier slowly closed his eyes and lay silent, gathering his strength.

Amo bolted over to Rachel and gathered her in his arms. "Rachel?" He sobbed, tears flowing unchecked onto her face.

Rachel's eyes fluttered, then opened.

"Why would you do such a stupid thing?" Amo whispered.

A sick smile smeared her lips across her face. "I love you, Amo," she said.

Amo's heart leaped at her words. He resolved to seal however long they had together with the truth. "I love you, Rachel," he said. The spark in her eyes gave him the courage to press on. "If you love me, Rachel, covenant to be my wife, binding yourself to me forever before the FINISHER and all of Spatium."

"I do," she whispered.

Amo took the ring of his father's house and pressed it onto Rachel's finger. He held her close and tenderly kissed her. A lumbering movement registered in Amo's peripheral vision, but it was too late.

"How touching!" Sier said. He lowered his head and charged toward them.

Amo pushed Rachel away just as Sier crashed into him,

sending them both rolling onto the deck of the Link. The brothers alternately wrestled and punched. They grunted and snarled, pounding each other's bodies in their fury.

Sier stood, extending his arms and preparing to land a crushing blow to his brother's back. Amo slid beneath Sier's legs and upended him, sending him flying.

Unbridled anger pulsing through his veins, Sier landed in a sprawling heap near where Rachel lay. An odious glint in his eye, he pulled her to himself.

"She deserves a fate far worse than your own!" He leered menacingly at Amo. "What true daughter embraces her own father's murderer?" Sier easily lifted Rachel's trembling body over his head.

"What true wife defiles her covenant, and shames her betrothed?" Sier bellowed.

"No, brother..." Amo barely breathed out the words.

For an instant, her terrified eyes met his. Then, Amo watched as Sier hurled Rachel away from the Link with all of his strength, into the utter blackness.

The crowd gasped, stunned—silenced by Sier's act of unfathomable cruelty.

"Nooo!" Amo let out a mournful, bloodcurdling cry.

Caduceus seized the moment of their hesitation; his voice affirming the deed. "Justice, though harsh, has been served!" He swept an inclusive arm over the crowd. "You have witnessed firsthand Rachel Spiritus' unfaithfulness and her careless disregard for the covenant that would have united the houses of Caasi and Spiritus!"

The mention of Caasi's and Spiritus' names reignited the crowd's fury. "Do not mourn this infidel," Caduceus bellowed. "Instead, recall her treachery and the injustice done to the venerable Spiritus!"

Caduceus artfully provoked the crowd to righteous indignation. "Rachel Spiritus has paid the ultimate price for her disloyalty and for bringing shame to her father's house!" He goaded the mob, whipping them into a frenzy of bloodlust.

Guards surrounded Riva, Sophia, and the council members who were loyal to her. The small contingent stood helplessly by as the miserable scene unfolded. Most cried. Many prayed for Amo and Rachel to be forgiven. The struggle to believe that the two could be guilty of such deception was visible on their faces.

Amo was unhinged with rage. A murderous look in his eye, he vowed vengeance on Caduceus and Hittitaes. Howling, he flew at his brother, intent on dispatching him.

Sier calmly waited, then fired a dense blast of pure energy directly at Amo's chest at point-blank range. The force of the impact tore Amo's mind from his body. He landed on his back, arms and legs splayed awkwardly on the glowing deck of the Link. Amo Caasi had been dispatched.

The crowd let out a resounding cheer. Shouting and celebrating, they hailed Sier as the victor and their deliverer. He had saved them from Amo, a traitor who had dared dispatch their beloved Spiritus. They chanted congratulations to Sier and Caduceus for discerning the deceitful heart of Rachel, and for rescuing Spatium from her treachery.

The euphoric celebration drowned out Riva's anguished weeping for Rachel and Amo, her lost children. Sophia and the others gathered about her, but she refused to be comforted.

And then, the light of the expanse began to dim. The air grew dark and foreboding. The cheering gradually quieted, replaced by whispers of fear.

"What is the meaning of this?" The whispering of the crowd grew

frantic. *"What's happening?"* The sound escalated into desperate cries as the shadows deepened, and all of Spatium became covered in darkness.

Suddenly, Amo's lifeless body began to glow. The light intensified until it shone with a brilliance that caused the Spatians to shield their eyes. After a moment, the light surged upward, hovering over Amo's body and dividing itself into three equally splendorous orbs. The first rocketed toward the expanse and out of sight, its radiance illuminating Spatium through the clouds. The second tore into the abyss, leaving an afterimage of pure light that cut a blinding gash in the inky blackness. The third luminescent sphere resettled into Amo, coursing through his veins and flooding his body with new life. He leaped to his feet as the eyes of the crowd widened in astonishment.

"Amo Caasi still lives!" A frightened voice yelled out.

Terrified, the crowd called on Sier to protect them.

"Save us!" the people cried. "Finish him! Finish him!"

The brothers ran at full speed, launching themselves bodily toward each other and colliding with an audible thud. Sier grabbed Amo and hurled him over the edge of the Link. The crowd gasped, certain Amo, too, had been lost to the abyss.

Amo managed to hang on to the side of the Link. He began pulling himself back up onto the deck.

"What has happened to you, brother?" he cried. "What about all that father taught us!" A tinge of sorrow colored Amo's voice.

"Shut up!" Sier shouted. "Don't lecture me about my father!" He swung, but Amo ducked and Sier missed.

Sier's momentum sent him lurching forward, arms pinwheeling, head first toward the abyss.

Amo spun barely fast enough to grab his brother's heels. He held on with all his strength. He strained with the effort, bracing his leg muscles against the side of the Link.

Suddenly, Sier's voice was soft. "Why keep holding on, little brother?" he asked. "Let me go." His words dripped with sorrow. "I grieve the loss of my father. I am estranged from my mother. Let me go, and you can have all that we've fought each other for."

"I am not your FINISHER, brother," Amo replied. "Your blood will not be on my hands." Amo held onto Sier's heels and with all of his strength, he launched himself backward and away from the edge of the Link. For an instant, Sier's bulk teetered between the abyss and the safety of the deck, before giving way to Amo's momentum.

The motion carried Sier up and onto the deck of the Link. His fingers clawed the smooth surface. Arms flailing, he leaped to his feet, knocking Amo over the edge.

Sier climbed up and turned to peer over the side of the Link.

Dangling by a handhold, Amo watched as his brother knelt above him on the deck.

"I love you, brother," Sier whispered.

Amo squinted up at Sier and slowly smiled. He heard the words of their father, Caasi.

"What will you choose when the time comes? Only one of you is destined to be Time-Ruler. Make your calling and election sure."

Amo looked deeply into his brother's eyes and then beyond them.

"I forgive you, Sier," Amo said. He let go of the Link and fell into the darkness of the abyss.

Follow:
www.SonsofCaasi.com

 @sonsofcaasi

 @cgrantsr

 www.facebook.com/SonsofCaasiSeries

Discussion Questions

1. Describe the dynamics between Caasi and Riva. Do they each have a relationship with the FINISHER? Give evidence to support your view.

2. How would you describe Sier's character? Is he a true villain? How does he change throughout the book? How do you think Sier responds to Amo's forgiveness?

3. What do you think is Amo's motivation for letting go of the Link? What do you think drives the attraction between Amo and Rachel? Does Amo achieve his goal of selfrealization by the end of the book? Why/ Why not?

4. What parallels can be drawn between Rachel and Hittitaes? How do you think the absence of their mothers impacts their character? Compare and contrast their relationships with their fathers.

5. What symbolism did you detect in the book?

6. Describe the family relationships in the House of Caasi. Can you think of other stories you've read with similar dynamics? How do those relationship dynamics drive the action of the story?

7. Identify and discuss some of the major themes/lessons from Battle for Time.

8. Choose a character and describe how he/she changes throughout the story.

9. Which character evokes the strongest emotional reaction (positive or negative) from you? Why?

10. Make a list of new words you discovered in the book. Write a brief definition that fits the context.

11. Much is made of Hittitaes' beauty. What effect do you think that has on her self-concept? On her relationships with others?

12. Why do you think the prophecies of the book of Fabula and Syuzhet are not readily decipherable to Caasi and the Royal Council of Spatium?

13. Describe what it might be like to exist outside of time.

14. While trying to make a difficult decision, Rachel recalls her mother, Aurora's words, "Great love sometimes requires even greater sacrifice." What do Aurora's words mean to you? Describe a time when you decided to make a personal sacrifice for the good of others. How did you arrive at your decision? What did it feel like to set aside your own plans or ambitions for someone else's benefit?

15. Why do you think Hittitaes uses Sier's ring to shoot Rachel at the Unveiling? Do you think she does it intentionally? Were you surprised when she used the ring against Counselor Spiritus? Why/Why not?

16. Choose a pivotal moment in the story and describe your reaction.

17. With which character do you most closely identify? What traits do you feel you share? Give evidence from the book to support your observations about the character you choose.

18. Discuss the significance of each of the following elements from the story: The Link, The Hall of Letters, Metasymbols

19. What was your gut reaction to Caduceus' speech to the crowd after Sier hurls Rachel from the Link? Could the crowd have responded another way? Explain your view.

20. How might the story have changed if Counselor Spiritus had lived to tell the Royal Council his revelation about the identity of Time-Ruler?

21. What do you think will happen as the story continues in the next book, "Reign of Deception"?

22. What do you think is the source of Amo's visions? What do you think the visions mean? What purpose might they serve in Amo's quest for self-realization?